IN THE
SHADOWS
OF DEATH

IN THE SHADOWS OF DEATH

Sourabh Mukherjee

Srishti
PUBLISHERS & DISTRIBUTORS

SRISHTI PUBLISHERS & DISTRIBUTORS
Registered Office: N-16, C.R. Park
New Delhi – 110 019
Corporate Office: 212A, Peacock Lane
Shahpur Jat, New Delhi – 110 049
editorial@srishtipublishers.com

First published by
Srishti Publishers & Distributors in 2015

10 9 8 7 6 5 4 3 2 1

This is a work of fiction. The characters, places, organisations and events described in this book are either a work of the author's imagination or have been used fictitiously. Any resemblance to people, living or dead, places, events or organisations is purely coincidental.

The author asserts the moral right to be identified as the author of this work.

Acknowledgements

I would like to take this opportunity to thank team Srishti Publishers for believing in my story. I would like to thank Wasim Helal for the engaging cover design, but most importantly for sharing my vision and being a part of the journey. Finally, many thanks to Moumita, my wife, for her keen and observant review of the manuscript, insightful feedback and creative inputs.

For more information about me and my books, visit http://www.facebook.com/authorsourabhmukherjee or https://in.linkedin.com/in/authorsourabhmukherjee, or write to me at thestoryteller1974@gmail.com.

Day 1
12:30 a.m.

A monsoon night towards the end of June, 2015
Central Plaza Hotel, Park Street, Kolkata

"Quite a dirty business, Agni," Inspector Arya Sen whispered to Agni Mitra, Assistant Commissioner of Police, Detective Department, Kolkata Police, as they made their way through the sparse crowd and headed for the toilets adjacent to the discotheque in the Central Plaza Hotel.

It was past midnight. The hotel in Park Street was not as crowded at that time of the night as it would usually be in the evenings. Footfall was low on a working day. Also with the restrictions on operating hours for pubs and discotheques across the city, the thin crowd at this time of the night was not a surprise.

The rumbles in the sky sounded ominous. It was raining outside, the dirt and grime on the busy roads washed off. Those who had run for cover under the shades included men and women who had been working late in the many offices in the neighbourhood, street children who would otherwise flock around foreigners staying in one of the plush hotels in the area, pimps who carried albums loaded with pictures of call-girls and would get in the way of men roaming around alone in Park Street, and hookers who roamed the streets or waited patiently for hours on end in desolate corners of the roads or in the bus stops in their loud make-up and hopeful eyes, waiting to be picked up and driven to cheap hotels around the place. The incongruous mix of people who stood next to each other, skin to skin, in the bus stops or under the ledges of the showrooms of global brands that lined the road, made Agni smile to himself every time he crossed them. That one stretch of road had something for everyone in the city – the movers and the shakers, and those resigned to the gutters.

Arya was bubbling with infectious energy, the hour of the night notwithstanding. It was a boon having Arya as a partner, Agni thought to himself yet again. Apart from the fact that Arya was one of the very few men in the force Agni got along with in the first place, Agni considered him one of the very few 'smart kids' the force had. He reminded Agni of his own early days in the force. Arya was always willing to walk the extra mile, thinking out of the box and had an eye for detail. Agni admired his aptitude for gathering and ingeniously analysing evidence. Arya's skills successfully complemented Agni's intuition, his deep understanding of the human mind and his style of getting into the psyche of a suspect rather than deliberating on material evidence.

"An undressed woman discovered dead in a toilet after an office party is dirty business indeed," Agni was his usual sarcastic self, as he stood at the entrance to the furthest stall in the line inside the ladies' toilet, his lean six feet frame almost towering over the crouching photographers busy taking pictures, his eyes fixed in the direction of the body that lay half-sitting on the floor inside.

Agni had of late been finding it increasingly difficult to make a guess at the age of female victims such as the one before his eyes, thanks to all the hard work most urban women put in to not look their real ages these days. But the one in front of him was definitely not beyond early thirties, maybe even younger.

The woman was in a sitting posture, her back resting on the wall, her legs folded at the knees. Agni imagined she might as well have been standing with her back against the wall and then slid down along the wall, landing on the floor on her bottom.

The shoulders were drooping, her hands hung loose on both sides of her body, the back of her palms touched the floor. The woman had a pink top on. Her blue denim pants were off. So were her panties. Both were bunched well below her knees. She had make-up on and her black hair was dishevelled. Her face was contorted, possibly with the pain her last moments had brought on her, part of the tongue hung out, and her large kohl-rimmed eyes almost popped off her pale but sharp-featured face. That beauty was history now.

Agni let out a sigh. Even after all these years in the force investigating murders, death still left him with a bad taste in the mouth.

"So what's this all about?" Agni turned to Arya, who had reached the crime scene almost an hour earlier and had made preliminary enquiries.

"There was an office party in the discotheque in the evening. The name of the company is Crescent Technologies. Their office is in Tech Park, the new IT hub in New Town. The victim has been identified as Sheetal Mehra. She worked for Crescent in Human Resources," Arya briefed Agni.

"And who found the body?" Agni asked.

"One of the ladies cleaning the restroom found the body, Agni. I have recorded her statement."

"What about the victim's family? Does she have any in the city? Has anyone been informed?"

"She stayed in a rented apartment with her husband at Elliot Road, not too far from here as a matter of fact. We found out his phone number from her office records. He has been informed."

Agni took another look around the stall and asked, "What did Doc have to say?"

"He is almost sure she was strangled to death. The autopsy will tell us more. He put the time between nine and eleven in the night."

"If the photographers are done," Agni glanced briefly at the men taking pictures, "let's seal this place off and send the body over for autopsy."

While stepping out, Agni examined the door and muttered to himself, "Doesn't look like anyone had to break in…"

As Agni stepped out of the restroom, his eyes caught one of the hotel staff outside the toilets and he stopped in his tracks. "Can I have a large black coffee please – with no sugar?"

"Certainly, sir," the man walked away. Agni seemed to remember something, turned around and added, "And please do bring me the bill."

Agni turned to Arya and said, "How many of her colleagues are here now?" He glanced at his watch.

"Only a handful of them are here, I'm afraid. Most of them had left by the time the body was discovered and the hotel authorities informed us."

Arya led Agni into the discotheque and introduced him to the handful of Crescent employees who were still around. He pointed to them and kept rattling off names – "Rajat, Priyanka, Ayushman, Sajid, Neelesh, Abhishek." Agni gestured to him to stop and watched the group intently. Most of them looked wasted from the heavy drinking all through the evening. Some of them looked exhausted from what must have been frenzied dancing on the floor, tees still drenched in sweat. They all looked shocked with the rather unexpected turn of events.

Agni said to Arya, "I don't want to hold everyone back too long. Make sure we have their statements and let them go. But they should realize that any Crescent worker who was in the party tonight is a suspect. And do let them know that they may be called up later for more elaborate questioning."

"Of course, Agni. The office executive, who made bookings for the party, is right here with a list of names of all those who were invited to the party. I had her come down here."

Agni looked at a rather distraught, bespectacled young woman who did look like she had been literally pulled out of bed at the unearthly hour. There was no sign of make-up. She had not had the time to do her shoulder-length hair. The floral print fuchsia dress was undoubtedly inappropriate for the occasion.

"Hello sir, I am Margarette. This is much unexpected and rather shocking for all of us."

Arya offered her a chair and signalled to one of the constables to get her a glass of water. "Well Margarette, murder always is. But we will make sure we let you go home and back to bed as soon as we can." The empathy was evident in Arya's voice.

"My colleague here tells me you have the names of people who were invited to this party?" Agni occupied a sofa right opposite Margarette and came straight to the point. Someone from the hotel staff had, in the meantime, placed on a low coffee table in front of Agni, a pot of black coffee, a cup and a saucer.

"I do, sir. I had received the names from Mr Vikrant Mittal... he heads the operations in Kolkata...and made the bookings at the hotel." She fished into her bag and pulled out a sheet.

Arya could see a long list of names printed in black with several strikethroughs and notes made in variously-coloured ink.

"I will keep this list with me for now. I'm sure you did an excellent job with the arrangements. The party, of course, didn't have to end the way it did. So were you in the party this evening, Margarette?" Agni poured some coffee into the cup from the pot and reclining on the sofa, took a sip.

"I wasn't, sir. I haven't been keeping well and didn't go to the office this morning as well."

"I'm sorry to hear that, Margarette. I will let you go for now. One last question before you leave. Is it possible to find out the names of those among the invitees who had actually turned up for the party?"

"I'm afraid that may not be possible, sir. The hotel doesn't have named reservations for a party like the one we had this evening. They had only asked for a headcount."

"I understand, Margarette. Thanks for your time and I will talk to you later."

Agni signalled to Arya to let her leave and then asked, "Do we have Mr Mittal here?"

"We do, Agni. He had left for the night but I had him called back here. Though he has been complaining for a while now and wants to be allowed to leave. It seems his blood pressure tends to be on the higher side and a sleepless night will do him no good," Arya sounded sarcastic.

"Guess what? An employee found dead in the loo with her pants off after an office party can do no boss any good," Agni shot back characteristically even as Vikrant Mittal approached him with an air of impatient arrogance.

"I am told you are in charge here. Well, can one of you record my statement and let me go? I have an early morning tomorrow with a client."

He was tall, handsome and spoke in a baritone that reverberated in the lounge almost startling everyone around him. His hair was greying at his temples and in his sideburns. He was sweating even with the air-conditioner on and was visibly restless. The stubble was more salt than pepper, the party shirt a bright purple.

"Well, just in case you haven't been involved in a police enquiry before, the officer in charge of the investigation is the one who decides when a murder suspect can be allowed to leave the crime scene. You really don't have a choice here," Agni sipped on his coffee, looking into Vikrant's eyes that widened with shock. He had not seen it coming.

"Excuse me? Did you say 'murder suspect'?" Vikrant's eyes narrowed. He was evidently not happy being tagged as one.

"You heard me right. Anyone who was in the party this evening is a suspect," Agni put the cup down. "Have a seat, please." He gestured towards the chair that had been vacated a while back by Margarette.

"You seem rather unperturbed by this very unfortunate incident, Mr Mittal. Your professionalism is laudable but it seems to me that your meeting with your client tomorrow morning is topmost in your mind right now, which I personally find rather odd." Agni made no attempt to hide his feelings.

"What is that supposed to mean? Of course the incident does bother me!" Vikrant retorted.

"I'm sure it does. We will not let you fall sick tonight, Mr Mittal, and we'll let you go after basic enquiries. But I may need you to come down to my office for more elaborate questioning later, and I want you to ensure that none of your colleagues who had been invited to this party this evening goes out of town till you are informed otherwise."

Vikrant was about to say something when Agni added without letting him speak, "Not even if it's for business that cannot wait. There can be no business more important than getting to the bottom of this."

"And what makes you think it's one of us?" Vikrant almost challenged the detective.

Agni smiled at Vikrant without bothering to reply.

"Arya, record his statement and let him go for now. Have a good one, Mr Mittal, and best wishes for your meeting tomorrow."

The husband had arrived in the meantime. He had walked up to the restroom, had taken a look at his deceased wife inside and had walked back to the lobby, sitting by himself without any visible display of his emotions.

"Agni, that's Abhinav Mehra, the victim's husband," Arya pointed out after he had recorded Vikrant's statement and let him leave.

Agni walked up to Abhinav and pulled a chair in front of him. Abhinav Mehra was remarkably calm. He had a light stubble, the hair a tad dishevelled and eyes reddish. Agni wondered if that was from grief, or simply because he had been woken up from sleep. He was in a grey T-shirt and black track pants, which might as well had been what he had worn to bed.

"Mr Mehra, I am in charge of this investigation. My name is Agni Mitra. I am sorry. This must be absolutely devastating for you."

Abhinav continued to look away.

Agni continued, "Well, this is neither the time nor the place, but procedure demands that I make basic enquiries. Would you mind telling me, Mr Mehra, where were you this evening when this most dreadful incident occurred here in this hotel?"

Abhinav remained silent for some time, as if to gather the strength to speak. And then he looked at Agni and said, "I had been in Mumbai on a business tour since last week. I reached Kolkata in the evening and came down to the hotel to pick Sheetal up from the party." He paused.

Agni bent forward, his eyes narrowing. "Do you remember what time in the evening that was?"

"It must have been around seven-thirty. I don't remember the exact time."

"Did you call her before you arrived at the hotel?" Agni asked.

"I did call her a few times while I was on my way, but she did not respond," Abhinav tried to remember the number of times he had called her.

"Didn't that strike you as odd?"

Abhinav looked up at Agni.

"No, not really. There was a party going on. They were all inside a discotheque. The music was loud. She might not have heard the phone. The phone might have been inside her purse, for that matter. There could be a lot of possibilities."

Agni leant back in his chair and closed his eyes. He then said almost in whispers, "Yes, you are right. There could indeed be a lot of possibilities."

Agni bent forward again.

"But you still came down to the hotel to pick her up?"

"Well...yes. I thought it would be quite a surprise for her. We had been very busy over the last several months. Since we both had the rest of the evening to ourselves, I thought it might be a good idea to make the most of it." For a fleeting moment, Agni thought he saw the pain in Abhinav's eyes.

"I do understand. And what happened next?"

'Well, I went up to the disco and met her there. But it seemed that the party had just started warming up and she wanted to stay back."

Abhinav looked away again.

"And you left without her?" Agni asked.

"Yes, I did. She said she might be late."

"Do you remember the time when you left the hotel?"

"Again, I do not recall the exact time. But, it must have been around eight."

Abhinav paused again and gulped. When he spoke again, his voice trembled.

"And then sometime back, I got this call from the police about...about her having been found in the restroom."

No words passed between the two men for a while.

Abhinav broke the silence with a whisper, "What a way to go!"

He stood up. So did Agni. "My condolences, Mr Mehra. As you can understand, we will need to take her away for conducting an autopsy. We will get in touch with you soon enough."

"I understand. If you have no further questions for me now, I would like to leave."

"Of course. I just wanted to let you know that you may have to stay in the city till I inform you otherwise."

"I understand, officer. I assure you of my co-operation in every possible way."

Abhinav paused, his jaws stiffening. "Sheetal did not have to die in a stinking toilet with her knickers off."

He walked away without looking back.

Over the next hour-and-a-half, Agni and Arya spoke to the few people from Crescent who had stayed back. Most of them had been too preoccupied in the party in their respective affairs to notice the rest. No one could recall for sure when they had last seen Sheetal and under what circumstances. The one common detail that came out of everyone's statement was that, of all her colleagues in the office, Sheetal was quite close to a certain Vaishali Arora.

When the last of them was gone and the body had been taken away for autopsy, Agni threw his arms back and stretched, with an audible creak from his stressed-out back.

"We don't really have a lot of material evidence and clues to go by here, do we?" He looked quizzically at Arya, knowing what interested him the most.

"I'm afraid we don't, Agni. We will have to wait for the autopsy report. I will also check the CCTV footages of people entering and leaving the hotel around the time of the crime. We should call up some of her colleagues at Crescent and start asking questions." Arya looked concerned.

"Yes. I'd especially want to talk to Vaishali Arora. She's the girl Sheetal spent the maximum time with during the party," Agni smiled and continued, "Bitching about the other girls or gossiping about the handsome boss. Gossip has a way of yielding vital clues."

Sometime in between, a member of the hotel staff had come up to Agni with the bill for the coffee and Agni had paid him.

Agni looked at his watch and turned to Arya. "Well, I'm done for tonight. What do you say we grab a couple of drinks at the bar before we head home?"

Agni had had plans of heading home earlier that night, but then, when had *he* been the master of his days and nights? And he had, since long, stopped complaining. It was rather ironic, he wondered at times, how malicious designs of evil men and women invariably shaped the course of his life. He was expecting a visitor in his apartment that evening, perhaps for the last time.

But it was too late, anyway. She would have left by now.

Day 1
04:00 a.m.

Agni watched the elevator door shut before he started on the twenty-one steps down the narrow corridor to the door of his twelfth floor apartment in a residential complex close to Lake Gardens, his senses numb from the whisky.

Like every night, the driver had offered to see him up to his apartment. Like every night, he had refused. Agni straightened his back and looked ahead in an almost defiant posture, inhaled the stale air of the corridor audibly through flared nostrils and walked the twenty-one steps to the door of his apartment.

On the twenty first step he stopped, and as expected, found himself right in front of the door with its brass knob. His tentative hands dived into the pockets of his trousers and managed to find the key. He inserted the key into the knob through the whisky mist, his head resting on the wooden door.

He heard the familiar click of the lock after the third attempt. That click brought a sense of relief. Yet another night when homicide investigator Agni Mitra made it to the safety and warmth of his house, inebriated, nevertheless functioning.

As he made his way in through the half-open door, Agni noticed the black heels, standing out among his gym shoes and a spare set of his duty boots.

He looked up. There she was, slouched at the dinner table with her back to him, her head buried in her arms. Agni's eyes hovered over her bare upper arm, a blue sleeveless kurta, a glimpse of a black bra strap on the shoulder. What was she doing in his apartment at this hour?

Agni took off his blazer and tossed it in the direction of the sofa. He did not bother to check where it landed. He made his way past the living area to the dinner table.

Agni looked back at her. She had not moved all this while. Agni wondered if she was asleep. Or maybe she was crying and did not want Agni to see her tears. She might even be dead. There was no way to tell.

Agni pulled a chair and sat down across the table. The lamp above the table was the only light in the room. Agni's eyes went to the shrivelled flowers in a vase on the table. The unintended symbolism was a crude reminder of what remained between them.

"Do you want something to drink? There should be some Diet Coke in the fridge," Agni asked Medha. Medha Chatterjee had been his wife till a week back.

Medha did not reply.

Agni walked up to the refrigerator and pulled out two cans of Diet Coke. His throat seemed parched. He pulled back the tabs from both cans and pushed one towards Medha.

"How long have you been here? Did you have dinner?"

Still no response.

"I had no idea you would wait for me!" Agni could not contain the surprise in his voice.

Medha raised her head finally and looked at the shrivelled flowers on the table. She took a sip from the can and said, "I didn't mean to. It doesn't make me particularly happy to see you. You know that, don't you?"

"Well, all I can see is you are here," Agni smiled wryly.

"You had said you would be home this evening. That's why I came down in the first place. I waited for you. It got late and I didn't want to go out." Medha paused and then said, "I'll leave in a while, don't worry about me."

The spare key was on the table. Medha had used it to get in. She pushed it towards Agni. "I don't think I'll need it anymore."

After another brief pause, Medha spoke again, "There's some packed Chinese food in the fridge in case you haven't had dinner. I ordered some for myself. And then I didn't feel like eating all of it."

Agni was not hungry. Not for Medha's leftovers, in any case.

"Why is she trying to be nice?" Agni thought to himself. "It is fashionable, perhaps, for ex-spouses to become friends, brushing aside the acrimony of several years that has pulled them apart in the first place."

"I had planned to come home earlier, you know. But there was this murder and I had to be there."

Medha looked straight into his eyes.

"You don't need to explain, Agni. I'm not your wife anymore."

She pushed the bra strap back under her dress. Anything she considered private was now out of bounds for Agni.

Agni went on, "A woman. Maybe your age. Killed in a loo. Quite depressing, really." Agni regretted it the moment he spoke. It was the whisky talking. He had no intention of opening up before that woman across the table. And he had ended up sounding almost apologetic about coming home late. Hell! The woman was right. She was not his wife anymore.

Medha kept looking at Agni.

"So homicide investigator Agni Mitra felt depressed again looking at a corpse?" she asked suddenly. Agni did not miss the hint of mockery in her voice.

"I did." Agni kept looking at the complicated thread-work on the table top. Every time he came home drunk and slumped on that table, the thread work on the table top assumed a new form, had a new meaning. "And you may want to be slightly more respectful towards a dead woman," he added.

"So you went drinking...to drown your depression?" Medha continued. "Isn't it surprising that it's the only way you can handle your emotions?"

Her voice had climbed a notch.

Agni wanted to get out of the conversation. He could do without the criticism.

Medha pushed the chair back and got up. "Well, as I had told you yesterday, in case you care to remember, I came down to get the rest of my stuff. Turned out there is far too much for me to carry back right now. I have packed them up. It would be kind of you if you can get a mover to deliver them to my address. You have my address, don't you?"

Agni considered whether he should offer carrying them over himself. And then he dismissed the thought. She was not his wife anymore. He had no business carrying around her stuff.

"Yes, I do," was all that he said.

"Well then. That's it. Sorry for messing up your night. You must have had a long day. Well, it's almost another day now." Medha looked outside. The darkness outside had started fading.

"About the divorce..." Agni took the last sip from the can of Diet Coke, holding it almost perpendicular to his face, and then brought down the empty can and placed it with a metallic clang on the glass table top, "nothing else remains to be done, I assume?"

"Nothing else. We are done."

"Was that it? It was quite easy, wasn't it? I had always thought divorce was a big deal."

"It isn't. Once you get over the mental barriers." Medha sounded characteristically dispassionate.

An awkward silence followed. And then Medha pulled the door shut and walked away. The sound of the door closing on his face almost startled Agni. And then the sound of her shoes down the corridor slowly faded away. And then he heard the elevator announcing its arrival with the familiar ding. He heard the elevator door close. And then the world around Agni fell silent.

Medha was gone. Agni would remember that moment for years to come.

Earlier that evening

Central Plaza Hotel, Park Street, Kolkata

*N*o sooner had she bolted the stall inside the ladies' restroom than she was all over me. She breathed warm and heavy as I brought my lips down on hers, impatiently sucking in first her upper lip and then the lower, saliva flowing between our mouths. I grabbed her by her hair as her lips parted, making way for my probing tongue and it slid into the vodka-scented warmth of her mouth. Our tongues wrestled and disengaged only when we were gasping for breath.

She cast a furtive glance towards the door. I saw fleeting reflections of a variety of emotions on her flushed face – surprise, apprehension, desire.

When I pulled her closer with an arm around her waist, her burning breath fanned my face. My nose and lips moved up and down the sides of her clammy neck. She had goosebumps all over. She shivered as I caressed her breasts over her top, a hiss escaping her mouth. I felt her deft hands all over me.

I unzipped her jeans in a jiffy and pushed it down past her knees. A throaty moan escaped her lips and she threw her head back. Her eyes were closed.

My hand got busy on her, where she needed me the most. As did hers on me.

Her eyes had been reduced to tiny white slits. My eyes were fixed on her face, reading its lusty contortions.

It was not too long before wave after wave of pleasure swept through her convulsing body. She had a sheen of sweat and her dishevelled hair was all over her face. The heat inside the stall was sweltering. She moved her hair off her face and kissed me hungrily. When she ended the kiss, she looked me in the eyes, and slurred, still trying to catch her breath, "God! What a surprise! What's come over you today?"

The noises inside my head got louder. Taking a couple of steps back, I looked long and hard at the woman in front of me writhing against the wall, still gasping in the throes of her release with her pants below her knees, wicked satisfaction painted all over her face, longing for my next move.

And what on earth was I doing there, standing and watching? If I did not act then, when would I ever act? The throbbing in my temples became unbearable and I closed my eyes. My fingers curled around her sweaty warm neck.

"You sure like it rough, don't you?," I heard her throaty moan drift into my ears.

My fingers tightened their grip on her neck.

"You are hurting me now. Go easy with this, okay?" she winced. The voice sounded feeble and was drowned by the heavy beats of the music playing in the party outside.

I was in no mood to oblige.

There was not a soul around as I zipped up and stepped out of the ladies' room and crossed the deserted corridor in brisk steps,

the music still playing loud inside the discotheque. I pushed the heavy door open and walked in. As I headed towards the sparsely crowded bar, I rolled my shirt sleeves down to cover the scratches. I thanked my stars that each one of her helpless kicks had missed my crotch by a whisker – the desperate last attempts at survival of a dying woman.

Sheetal Mehra was dead.

Day 1
5:00 p.m.

Arya and Agni were seated across the table facing Vaishali Arora in Agni's office. Agni sipped on black coffee.

Vaishali was in her early thirties, and in noticeably good shape. She was in jeans and a kurta that was almost a second skin. Her hair was neatly tied back and she wore fashionable spectacles. Her eyes behind those spectacles, however, looked tired and Agni felt there was a general air of melancholy about her demeanour.

She had apparently come down to the police station straight from her office and had not bothered to remove the ID. Agni stole a glance at her picture on the ID. She did not look particularly cheerful in that picture as well, just a few years younger.

Arya spoke first. Agni always left the introductions to Arya. That was an undocumented contract between the two men.

"Well, thanks Ms Arora, for making the time. I have a fair idea about the kind of hours you probably spend in the office. A cousin of mine has been an IT professional for several years now, and I honestly don't remember when we last spent an evening together. I know the time you spend here with us will probably delay your return home further tonight." Arya sounded almost apologetic. The girl in front of him looked sad and vulnerable and he was yet to master the art of not letting his emotions get in the way of conducting an enquiry.

Agni cast a cold stare in his direction that silenced him immediately. *Cold as steel. Purely analytical. No emotions.* Arya reminded himself of Agni's mantra for effective interrogations.

"That's okay. Sheetal was a friend and I want to make sure we get to the bottom of this at the earliest." For a few seconds Vaishali looked away, outside the window to her left.

"And you can call me Vaishali." She looked back at the two policemen.

"I believe you spent a lot of time with Ms Sheetal in the party that evening, Vaishali?" Agni asked, his head thrust back on the chair, his legs crossed under the table.

"Yes, we were usually together in every office party."

"Did you see Sheetal with anyone else that evening for sufficiently long?"

"It was an office party and there were a lot of people. It's very difficult to remember everything. I remember Ayush…Ayushman Dutt, he is a colleague…spent some time with us. Then, the new girl in HR…I think she said her name was Shalini…joined us for a couple of drinks. And of course, Abhinav came down to meet Sheetal."

"I see. Since when have you known Ms Sheetal?"

"We knew each other even before we started working for Crescent. We were in college together. We were in different streams, though. In Crescent, she worked in the HR department. I am a part of the Technology team. In fact, Abhi was also in our gang in college."

"Abhi?"

"Oh, I meant Abhinav, Sheetal's husband. Have you met him?"

"Yes, we have met. He was remarkably in control of his emotions that night."

"Yes! Abhi is not very expressive. In fact, it came as a surprise to all of us when the two of them went ahead and got married. None of us in college had a clue!"

"And why were you surprised?" Agni bent forward, his eyes narrowed.

Vaishali remained silent for a few minutes. She was visibly uncomfortable about something. Agni could not put his finger on it that very moment, but he made a mental note. He would need to re-visit that note later.

And then she spoke, as if after she had managed to put her thoughts together. "They were very different individuals. In fact, none of us had the slightest idea that Abhi was in love with *her*."

"Are you suggesting that your friends, and probably you, had thought that he was in love with someone else? You seemed to have stressed on that last word," Agni smiled.

Vaishali was quiet again with her eyes fixed on Agni's coffee mug on the table. When she looked up, she did not look at Agni for quite some time. Continuing to look outside at the slowly descending darkness, she almost whispered, "Maybe they shouldn't have married in the first place. Abhi took an impulsive decision, I guess."

"And why do you say that?"

"I don't think they ever got along too well. Abhi has a job that keeps him away from home for months on end. Sheetal was very lonely."

"I can imagine. And did she confide in you?"

"Yes, she did. She was looking for stability. She needed support. She was looking for a man who would stand by her. And she started seeing a lot of men."

"Because she was lonely? But that never helps, does it?" The situation seemed uncannily familiar to Agni.

"You are right. That doesn't help. And I did warn her. But she did not listen to me. She said she would end her marriage the day she found someone worth it. She used to say she would be cautious while getting into a steady relationship again and would wait for the right man. But she didn't pretend that she would not kiss every frog that came her way. And there was never a dearth of men for Sheetal."

"She was indeed a gorgeous woman," Agni chose not to remember the macabre scene in the ladies' toilet where he had first seen Sheetal. Some of her photographs he had seen later were the ones he would choose to remember her by, any day.

"Was there anyone from the office…I mean, among the men Ms Sheetal was dating?" Agni looked into Vaishali's eyes.

She replied, "Well, she hinted at a few affairs in the office, but she never took names. And I did not insist either."

"I completely understand. By the way, while we are on the topic of marital woes, if you don't mind my asking, Vaishali, are *you* married?"

"No, I'm not. And I'm not sure how that information could be of any help to this investigation."

"Well, one never knows." Agni smiled. "So, coming back to the subject of our discussion, you said Ms Sheetal was going around seeing random men. Was Mr Mehra aware of this?"

"He was suspicious. You know, as they say, the spouse always gets wind of these matters."

"They indeed do." Agni was quiet for a few seconds. He needed that time to wipe out the disturbing images forming in his mind. There was no way he could let his own perspectives on relationships influence his questions.

Vaishali broke the silence this time. "In fact, they had a fight in the party that evening."

"You mean Ms Sheetal and her husband?"

"Yes, he had come down to the hotel on his way home from the airport to pick her up. But she refused to leave with him. That got him upset."

"But it was an office party. What was he upset about?"

"She was drunk and my guess is he had seen her dancing very close with a couple of guys when he had walked in."

"Did you overhear their conversation or did Ms Sheetal tell you about the fight herself?"

"I did not overhear them. The music was loud. The place was crowded. And I was on the dance floor, quite far from them. But I saw them talking. The conversation looked very animated. I could make out they were shouting at each other. And later, Sheetal told me that they had had a fight."

"And then, did you see Mr Mehra leave after Ms Sheetal had chosen to stay back in the party?"

"You know what? I didn't see him leave. I don't remember now what exactly happened. I think Mr Mittal called me to introduce someone. And after sometime, when I saw Sheetal again, she was by herself, drinking at the bar. We talked for a while and then I left."

"Do you remember when you left the party that night?"

"I guess it was after eight, maybe a quarter past. Sheetal said she would stay back for a while. She was quite drunk by the way and I was worried for her even as I left."

"And that was the last you saw of her?"

"Yes."

"How did you get to know about her death?"

"Abhi called me later that night after he had returned from the hotel the second time…after he had seen her dead, you know. I couldn't believe what I heard."

"Yes, it must have been quite shocking for you. And I sincerely hope it won't be long before we find out who did it, Vaishali."

"I hope."

Vaishali looked at her watch and said, "I should leave now if you have no more questions. I am getting late for a meeting in the office."

Agni looked at his watch. "Oh yes! It's quite late. We won't keep you any longer. You have been very helpful, Vaishali. And please don't hesitate to get in touch, should you remember anything that you feel could be of help or if you want to discuss something with us."

"Of course," Vaishali smiled dryly at the two men and walked away.

Agni turned to Arya. "What do you think, Arya? If, of course, you could divert a fraction of your attention to the case we have on our hands, from appreciating the charms of the lady."

Arya's flushed face betrayed his embarrassment. And he hurried to make up by offering his opinion.

"I did notice a few things in her behaviour, Agni, which I found rather strange."

"Such as?" Agni looked appraisingly at Arya. His legs were uncrossed and he was bent over the table, his fingertips joined in an arch.

"She was not comfortable when you asked her if the gang of friends in college was under the impression that Abhinav was in love with someone else."

"Excellent observation! I'm impressed. I noticed that, too. What else did you find interesting?"

"I also made note of the fact that she did not see Abhinav leaving the hotel that night after he had been mad at his wife over her behaviour in the party. In fact, of all the people we have spoken to, very few mentioned his being in the discotheque that night in the first place. And none of them had seen him leaving the hotel."

"I know. Those are good points you make there, Arya. Also, there could have been those men from the office Sheetal was dating, or those she had dated in the past and dumped."

Agni was quiet for a few minutes. He then spoke in whispers, "We have here at least two individuals who had been dealt the wrong hand by destiny. A woman who probably lost her love to her friend and a man trapped in a bad marriage witnessing the errant ways of his wife. Not to mention the possibility of having a few more jilted admirers around in that party.

"Crimes of passion can be nasty sometimes, Arya."

Day 2
10:00 a.m.

Abhinav Mehra looked remarkably calm for someone coping with a personal loss. With a cursory acknowledgement of Agni's condolences, he took his seat and cut to the chase immediately.

"As you may be aware, Officer, I head the sales operations for my company and my work demands frequent travels to offices of my clients who are spread all over the country. The restriction on my travels is not helping the business."

"I don't doubt. But, you do realize that we need to go by the book. There has been a murder, an investigation is in progress, and irrespective of whether you find this palatable or not, you are a suspect.

"I would only request you to co-operate with us, so that we get to see the end of these difficult times soon enough. And if your innocence is proved beyond doubt, you'll be free to board the next flight out of town. Makes sense?" Agni reclined on his chair, as if he had put a deal on the table for Abhinav.

Abhinav did not hide his exasperation. He threw his hands up in the air and resigned, "As if you leave me a choice." He seemed to reflect on Agni's soliloquy for a few seconds and followed that up with, "A murder suspect – *me?*"

"That indeed is the sad reality, Mr Mehra."

A potent silence followed in the room. And then Agni spoke, "So let's start from the start, shall we? How long were you married, Mr Mehra?"

"A little more than five years."

"And how long had you known Ms Sheetal before you married her?"

"We studied together."

"Same school? Same college? Same friends?"

"Same college. Yes, we had quite a few common friends. Not sure if you've met Vaishali Arora from Sheetal's office. She was a common friend."

"We've certainly met her," Agni confirmed.

"Nothing is too personal in a murder investigation, Mr Mehra. So, would you mind telling us if all was well with your marriage?"

"Thanks for the subtlety," Abhinav smirked in sarcasm. He paused for a few minutes, taking a sip from the glass of water that had been placed before him, and then began thinking with his head down. He took time choosing his words so that his statement did not outrage any further a relationship, the festering sores of which had been exposed to the world a couple of nights back in the toilet of a hotel.

"Well…we were very young when we got married. We fell in love and got married within months of discovering our feelings for each other. In fact, most of our friends were surprised too. They had had no clue about what had been brewing between us. Not even Vaishali…considering she was very close to both of us."

"How did the problems begin?" Agni had been listening intently.

"Our lives got complicated. As I mentioned to you, my job entails frequent travels across the country and abroad. We never had a stable marriage. Sheetal was not happy with my staying away from home most of the time. At the same time, she could not accompany me in my travels as she had her own work in Kolkata. The fights became more frequent and the two of us drifted apart. The situation got worse over the last couple of years. Sheetal was lonely and gave in to temptations. I don't really blame her. Somewhere I blame myself for this tragic outcome of my marriage, Officer. I should have read the warning signs long back."

As he took notes, Arya could not but appreciate Abhinav's attempt to take a stand for his failed marriage. It was as if Abhinav had decided to grab that one last chance he had to respond to all the aspersions against his deceased wife. But then, from whatever Arya had seen over the years, that might as well be a carefully crafted façade. One could never be too sure.

Agni had been listening to Abhinav with his eyes closed. He spoke up few minutes after Abhinav had stopped. "You never suspected anything, Mr Mehra?"

"To be honest with you, Officer, I did find her behaviour suspicious on a few occasions. But I deliberately chose to keep negative thoughts at bay. In fact, there were times when I hated myself for harbouring such thoughts about Sheetal. Also, I never had any evidence to confirm my doubts."

"And you never discussed your doubts with your wife?"

"Well...she never mentioned anyone. And I didn't ask."

"What happened that evening?"

"As I had told you that night, I had been on a business tour in Mumbai the week before. That evening, I took a taxi from the airport to the hotel to pick her up on my way home. She refused to leave the party and said that she would be late."

It seemed Abhinav wanted to say more, but Agni sensed an ever-so-slight hesitation. He bent forward, his arms on the table, his fingertips forming an arch as he looked straight into Abhinav' s eyes. "It was not so easy a conversation, was it?"

For the first time since he had stepped into the room, Abhinav looked unsettled.

"What do you mean, Officer?"

"You heard me, Mr Mehra. It's in your best interest to tell me what exactly transpired between Ms Sheetal and you that evening. Let's wind the spool back a bit, shall we? What did you see when you entered the disco?"

"Well, the party was on. Unfortunately not too many of her colleagues know me. I don't really socialize with them—"

"I hope you understand I'm more interested to know about Ms Sheetal. We can discuss her colleagues in more amiable circumstances." Agni smiled.

"I saw her on the dance floor."

"Alone?"

Abhinav almost glared back at Agni. Agni was his composed self, the smile glued at the corner of his lips. He reclined on the chair. "I told you Mr Mittal, there's nothing too personal in a murder investigation. We want to get to the bottom of this."

Abhinav looked away. With his eyes fixed on the tiled floor of the police station, he said almost in whispers, "There were a few of her colleagues...male colleagues. And when she spoke to me, it seemed she had had a few too many shots of the vodka."

Agni did not move his eyes off Abhinav. Agni saw the colour changing on his face. His cheeks were flushed. What was it? Embarrassment? Anger? Hatred for the dead wife? Agni would have to push the probe deeper. He would have to carry Abhinav back in time, right inside that dimly-lit smoke-filled discotheque. He brought his face very close to Abhinav's and asked, "And what did you feel at that very moment, Mr Mehra?"

Abhinav looked up from the floor, hint of a tear at the corner of an eye, his face contorted with pure hatred. He grimaced, his voice climbed several notches. "That night, I wanted to listen to the voices in my mind, Officer, which I had been ignoring for months. I had lost Sheetal, and the truth was out there for me to see, for everyone to see...right there in front of my eyes. *I had never felt more angry and more humiliated all my life.*"

"Now now, Mr Mehra, be careful! Those are very strong words!" Agni's steel claws were out and they had sunk into Abhinav's bleeding wound even before he realized it. The despair, the anger vanished from Abhinav's face, draining it of all its colour. Arya had never seen someone turn deathly pale from a livid red so fast.

Abhinav drank from the glass of water, took a deep breath and tried to pull himself together. He regretted giving vent to his pent up emotions. Suddenly, he found it difficult to maintain his poise. He felt vulnerable, stripped before the prying eyes of the hawk in front of him, its shadow now looming large over him. In that battle of nerves, he had allowed Agni to overpower him.

Agni resumed. "So what did you finally decide to do? Leave your wife with the pack of wolves?" Agni smirked.

Abhinav thumped on the desk. "Why are you doing this to me? She is dead, for God's sake." The anger was back and with that a hint of helplessness. The tears spilled over.

"She did not *choose* to die, Mr Mehra. Someone pushed her to that death. Someone who felt that was the death she deserved. Violated in a dirty toilet. *Someone very angry with her.*" Agni stood up and paced up and down the room, uttering each word with gnawing brutality, his deep voice reverberating in that small room.

Abhinav's defences were fast giving away. He was beginning to feel like a rag doll getting soaked. "I…I left the hotel and returned home," he managed to say.

"In the same taxi? I am assuming you were not in the hotel for too long?"

"Yes…yes, I wasn't there for long."

"Did you park the taxi inside the hotel?"

"Well, no. It was parked outside the hotel. I had thought it wouldn't take too long…"

"I understand. You left the hotel around eight, if I remember what you told me that night?"

"Yes, well, I didn't check the time. But it must have been around eight," he added a feeble, "I guess".

"And did anyone see you leaving?"

"I'm not too sure. As I told you, not many of her colleagues know me."

"Ah! There goes your alibi out of the window!" Agni thumped a fist on the other palm, in mock frustration. Abhinav's heart skipped several beats as he looked up alarmed, eyes wide, mouth gaping.

Agni continued, "Vaishali Arora must have been in the party, too. She is your friend, isn't she? Didn't you bother to say hello to her?"

"Of course, she's a close friend. But we didn't meet that evening. She wasn't with Sheetal when I stepped in."

"I can imagine. You had far more important issues to deal with that evening than socializing with college buddies," the sarcasm stung Abhinav where it hurt the most.

"And then, going by your earlier statement, the police called you back later that night to the same hotel."

Abhinav had lost the strength to speak. He nodded weakly.

"And am I to believe that for the entire time in between, you were home?"

"I was."

Agni seemed lost in thought, a few wrinkles on his forehead. After a while, he looked up and said, "One last question, Mr Mehra. When was the last time you spoke to Vaishali?"

Abhinav replied, "I called Vaishali after returning home from the hotel the second time. I wanted to find out if she already knew about the incident and if she could throw some light on what might have happened to Sheetal inside that hotel. It turned out that I was the one breaking the news to her!"

The wry smile was back on Agni's face. "I perfectly understand, Mr Mehra. You may leave now. Thanks for your time." A feeble shake of hands followed.

When Abhinav walked out of the room, Agni turned to Arya, the corner of his mouth curved in a smile.

"We got but a glimpse of the inner recesses of Abhinav's mind, Arya. But, that was enough for me to put him near the top of my list of suspects.

"You never know how many more such closed rooms we need to break into."

Day 2
10:00 p.m.

Back in his apartment, Agni took a cold shower. He realized the house was fast running out of supplies. He cursed himself under his breath. He had to get used to a life without Medha.

He heated up the Chinese food he had picked up on his way. Staring at the vacant chairs around the dinner table, he was suddenly too conscious of his solitude. And then, Agni had to remind himself he had decided not to think about Medha.

At the same time, he tried to figure out what in his line of sight looked more pathetic – the shrivelled flowers in the vase, or those empty chairs? He stood up swiftly and picked up the vase with the shrivelled flowers and headed for the trash bin.

Over the last few days, Agni had looked around in the house. Medha's bottles of perfume, nail polish, moisturizers and lotions, her dryer, hair-straightener, all her pills, her ridiculously large collection of watches, shoes and bags, her undergarments – everything was gone. Not even the faintest smell of Medha remained in Agni's house. The clutter Agni had gotten used to over the years had suddenly been wiped out. She had calculatedly removed from the shelves all the books and CDs that either she had bought for herself or Agni had gifted her.

Agni had looked at the old photo albums, those priceless collections of pictures the two of them had spent hours putting together before digital photos surrounded human beings in all directions in the ether. Those pictures brought back pleasant memories – and then, the unpleasant ones. Both hurt equally. That probably was why she had chosen to leave those albums behind in the first place. To draw fresh blood from his wound every time he looked at those pictures. Agni had no choice but to accept it, as he did not have the heart to throw those pictures away. That would not have erased her memories in any case.

Agni suddenly lost his appetite. Dumping the dishes in the kitchen sink, he headed for the balcony with the bottle of whisky.

Looking back, Agni wondered how they had managed to spend those four years together in the first place. Two individuals, so very different. They had probably been experimenting with marriage on fragile grounds – a half-hearted experiment at that.

Agni had been spending his days away from home pretty much round the clock, losing himself in his investigations. The holidays had become few and far between, the odd weekend movies had become exceptions, the love-making a check in the box. And then there was, of course, the child that Agni had kept denying Medha all those years.

Agni doubted if he would be able to stand as fearlessly before the gun of an assailant without a care in the world once he had kids waiting for him back home. He had also felt that having kids in the hood would curb his freedom, put restrictions on the way he lived his life, a day at a time.

He had talked Medha out of having the baby when it had come along in the second year of their marriage. He did not even remember the pretexts he had come up with to justify himself. He had probably spoken about his work schedules and her career as an interior decorator that had just started taking shape. He had probably talked about the need for better earnings for a bigger family. He had probably spoken about the need for a bigger house. He had probably reasoned that the two of them needed more time to themselves before a child could be allowed to take up bed-space between them on the second year of their marriage. But he knew that none of those arguments had been true. It was just his fear of having kids.

Medha had conceded. What Agni had not expected was that by denying her the child Medha had wanted so badly, he had unconsciously put himself in emotional debt to her. Every time he looked at her, he felt guilt and his conscience pricked at his innards. The power equation in the relationship had changed, but in a way Agni had not foreseen.

What he had celebrated as a personal victory soon gave way to his biggest defeat. He started staying away from her. His work became his getaway. Medha became lonelier than ever, even as she battled alone the grief of losing an unborn child.

Medha kept herself busy with her work. Her home decoration business flourished. The money started flowing in. And the men, mostly rich, young, bored, and with deep pockets, who consulted her to decorate their fancy apartments. Men who had seen too much of success too early in life and did not have much to look forward to, seeking quick gratification in pleasures of the flesh. Medha found herself not turning down the propositions. And then, she started seeking them out. She was not lonely anymore. Also, perhaps, it was her way of getting back at Agni for his consistent negligence of her emotional and physical needs – not being aware, at the least, of the inner devils that Agni himself was battling.

Agni remembered the evening he had chanced upon Medha's mobile phone in the bedroom. Medha herself was in the living room watching TV. The phone vibrated silently at short intervals as messages kept pouring in. Agni reached for the phone and then hesitated. Would that not be snooping on his wife? Was it not all about trust? And then his curiosity won over his sense of propriety.

He unlocked her phone with the familiar pattern and read those messages, sitting at the edge of the bed. When he stood up, the room seemed to whirl around him. He reached out for the nearest wall to steady himself.

When he walked up to the living room, he saw her watching TV, her legs stretched out to the low coffee table in front of the couch. It did not look like she was enjoying whatever she was watching. She yawned frequently. He stood in front of her, the lamp behind casting his long shadow that engulfed her.

"You want something? Some coffee? I could do with one myself. This story is not going anywhere," Medha stood up.

Agni's heart pounded and there was a knot in his throat as he searched for words.

"This indeed is not going anywhere," he muttered and walked up to the open door that led to the balcony. He fervently hoped that his face did not betray the pain he felt in his heart. The woman he had naively assumed to be devoutly monogamous was now hiding behind her mask, playing the part like a seasoned professional.

"I didn't hear you," she said a couple of times.

Agni tried to get his voice back. And then he turned and walked towards the wardrobe.

"I need to go to the station. Just remembered something I should have taken care of," he managed.

"Agni, I probably shouldn't say this as I know you don't like me interfering with your work, but what you are doing with your life..." Medha paused for a few seconds, "is...is wrong. This is going to affect your work in the long run."

Agni turned to her trying to force a disdainful smile. "Medha, I am the best at my work. I do it by getting into the minds of people. And I do it well." His eyes narrowed. The steel cold stare bored into her. "I sometimes read people wrong in my private life though."

If Medha's heart skipped a beat, it did not show on her face.

Agni walked out, slamming the door behind him.

And Medha continued to sleep around with random men. Agni never bothered to find out how many or with whom. Agni had reasoned with himself – that was perhaps the price destiny made him pay for talking his wife into aborting their baby.

The fate of their marriage was in Medha's hands and then she made her choice. She wanted to end the marriage. She felt that would take the guilt away and make her feel free. It would save her the arduous task of having to cover her tracks and devise ingenuous lies every time she slept with someone. That was what her life had become – a life of lies.

It was a sultry evening in the summer. One of those rare ones when Agni was home. He was in the balcony sipping a can of beer and she was in the bedroom with her laptop.

She came out of the bedroom in her grey top and purple shorts with her hair open, and stood at the door leading to the balcony from the dining hall. That's when she announced that she wanted a divorce.

"It's your choice, Medha. It's what *you* want," Agni said, his unseeing eyes fixed on the evening traffic progressing at its lethargic pace on the dusty road below.

"What about you? I'm asking you," she seemed to check.

"What about me?" Agni took a long slug of the beer and turned to face her. "No. I'm not fine with it. But, I cannot hold you hostage in this marriage, can I?"

"You do realize this marriage isn't going anywhere, don't you?" she tried to reason.

"You sure seem to be going places." Agni looked away from her at the heavy, dark clouds in the horizon, looking almost ready to burst any time.

The hint was not lost on Medha. So he knows, she thought to herself, what else can you expect when you are married to a cop?

"Yes, I am. With real men who know how to make a woman happy," Medha decided she was not going to be defensive about this.

Agni interrupted her with a smirk, "Happy in bed, you mean."

"And why would *you* care?" Medha retorted.

"Which means I was right after all," Agni muttered under his breath, taking a sip of the beer.

"Agni, I need a life. I need a life that I don't have to feel sorry and ashamed about," Medha shouted, a crow perched on the railing of the balcony took off.

"You look anything *but* ashamed of your life right now," Agni finished the beer.

And that was it. The foundations they had laid in their marriage over the past four years had been shaky. It had been but a matter of time before it collapsed.

Agni came back to the present. Everything he had heard about Sheetal and Abhinav from Vaishali in the police station the day before had seemed familiar. Agni now knew why.

He thanked his stars that he had never had to *see* his wife drunk and in the arms of other men. Being part of such a scene in reality had to be worse than imagining one.

He headed towards his dark, cold, lonely bedroom. Life in the shadows of separation and death was a bitch.

Day 2

You clap around a mosquito buzzing around in the air conditioned comfort of your car and it dies right away. Now that isn't a whole lot of fun, is it? You end up with a blood stain and the shapeless, lifeless remains of a blood-sucker squashed on your hands. That's about it. The end. No drama.

Now consider this. The mosquito doesn't die right away. Maybe you didn't get the angle right. Maybe not enough force to kill. But enough to make it land on the dashboard, dismembered. Maybe a leg torn off. The flight interrupted. And you watch it crawl on the dashboard. Trying to fly. Trying to escape the imminent death staring it in the eyes. And failing every time. And then you get into action. You chop a wing off and then perhaps another. Maybe a couple more legs go next. And in your mind, you clap in glee as you see its mutilated form crawl around, the taste of your blood it sucked a while back still fresh in its mouth, still holding on to its impossible hope of flying out of what would be a miserable death.

Now, how far have you gone? Have you ever gone to the extent of snipping off all its legs and wings but taking care not to kill it? I did that just now, as the traffic signal remained red.

What a sight! The life slowly ebbing away, all the hope of flight slowly vanishing. Till I finally squeezed his life out between my fingers. Right there, on my dashboard.

There are so many ways to keep yourself entertained when you are caught in a red light. But nothing beats the joy of relishing slow but certain death.

The mosquito lying dead on my dashboard reminded me of the human beings I have seen dying. Too hurt, too breathless, too helpless but still fighting. The urge to live was universal. So was the urge to suck each other's blood. Nothing beats the joy of seeing someone suffer.

The traffic signal was still red and counting down. There were school children crossing the road – girls in their white shirts, blue skirts, plaits and happy faces. I kept looking at them, and remembered her. The year was 1999 and I was fifteen. A summer afternoon.

The hum of the fan was the only sound that reached my ears. The heat was sweltering, and the humidity made it worse. The windows of all the houses around mine were shut tight. Haggard dogs on the road had their tongues out and crows moved around restlessly with gaping mouths. I could see rickshaw pullers catching a nap under the hoods, and an ice-cream seller wiping his brow and looking around expecting accidental business. The only other trace of life on that deserted road was a man pushing in coloured leaflets, probably about a new Chinese restaurant or about someone who believed he could repair refrigerators and television sets, into worn-out letter boxes that added to the ugliness of the front walls of the buildings around me. My

heartbeats were growing more disconcerted with each passing minute.

And then, from my first floor window, I saw the bus. That flash of yellow paint, worn out here and there revealing the rusty iron underneath, my eyes had been yearning for. I saw it turn the bend at the far end of the dusty road and then slowly make its way between rows of dreary old houses, to stop a few feet from where a small flight of stairs rising from the pavement led to our front door. I could not wait to inhale the smell of exhaust fumes from that rickety old school bus, which had seen better days. That was the bus of St Mary's Girls' School. No one waited for that bus at that hour of the day all year like I did.

Because that was the time when I got to see her. And even if I dozed off, there was an alarm clock that would wake me up sharp at three. I never managed to wake up on time in the mornings to see her board that bus on her way to school. I had no idea where exactly she lived. There would often be those unexpected and hence all the more exhilarating glimpses of her on the road ahead, but one could not rely solely on chance in matters of the pining heart.

She was pretty much the same age as me. Her face was a perfect oval with black eyes that talked. Her hair used to be meticulously tied back in a ponytail. Her crisp white shirt would be tucked neatly into her blue skirt that reached just below her knees. The white socks would reach just above her ankles. She would have a handkerchief clutched in her hand. There would be sweat glistening on her temples as she got down from the bus. She would say her 'byes' to boisterous boys and girls inside the bus, standing there with her satchel and waving at them till the bus groaned its way out of sight. And I would keep praying that she look back at me – just once. She would not. She never did.

And I lived my days and my nights with that one imaginary scene playing in my mind's eyes like a videotape on loop. I spent hours every day, like I had been doing a while back, drawing her pictures. On that dusty road with her satchel on her back, her head turned in my direction, her eyes catching my gaze. I imagined a wind out of nowhere on that dusty road playing with the strands of her hair on her face, as dirt circled up towards the heavens. I only hoped that my feelings showed in my eyes. If only she looked at my eyes. But she never did. Those sketches piled up.

After getting down from the bus, she would cross the road and make her way through the narrow lane right opposite to my house, which meandered through shabby old buildings that almost breathed on each other. I had no idea where she came from and where she vanished every afternoon down that lane.

That afternoon, before entering that lane, she turned round. She must have seen me watching! I could not breathe for the next few minutes. It felt like someone had just sucked the air out of my innards and my heart thumped so loud I was afraid she would hear it. I stuck my face out of the window till the iron grills would not let me any further.

"This finally is my day," the words escaped my mouth.

And then I saw what I had never imagined I would see.

She looked to her left, then to her right, then after an unseeing glance upwards, sweeping across the closed windows of the houses on my side of the road, waved at someone on the road below with a smile, stealthily blew a kiss and then started running down that lane.

I don't know even to this day who that kiss was meant for. I could not see him from my window. But I could feel a searing pain slowly taking me in its grip. I had the drawing pencil in my right hand. I pressed the tip of that pencil so hard on my thigh that the tip broke. The shock gave way to a sense of defeat, which gave way to helplessness and eventually made way for extreme rage.

When I looked up again, the world before me was a blur as tears rolled down my cheeks.

I saw a lot of her over the next few years. Even after that fateful afternoon, I would find myself rooted near the window everyday for a glimpse of the girl who would never turn her head and look a few feet above the ground at me. My hope never left me. But I still could not muster the courage to walk the few steps down to the road ahead and talk to the girl with whom I talked in my imagination for hours, every day and night.

I saw her on days when she got down from her bus triumphantly with trophies in her hand and on those when she got down from the bus with a long face. I saw how over the years she filled out her school uniform. I saw her on days when she got down from the bus only to get on someone's bike. Quite a few boys over the years, in fact. I would see her speed away down that road with her face covered in a scarf, with her arms around a different boy every few months.

My dreams, which used to keep me up night after night, and found expression only in my sketches over the years, began to look more impossible with every passing year. And as she probably lost count of the number of boys she went out with, my frustration snowballed into extreme rage. I could almost visualize my dreams hitting the ground and licking the dust, never to get back on their feet again.

I realized to my dismay that even if I did manage to overcome my awkwardness, even if I did manage to walk down that flight of stairs, even if I did manage to speak to her and win her attention, my days of glory would surely be numbered. I knew that for sure.

I had not noticed when the lights had turned amber and then green. I was pulled out of my memories by cars honking behind me. Memories of my first crush, also my earliest recollections of the wanton ways of a woman.

At fifteen, I had no idea that my nightmare had just begun.

Day 3
11:30 a.m.

"Catch your breath, Arya," Agni gestured towards the glass of water on his table. "Here, help yourself."

Arya pulled a chair and sat right opposite to Agni, his excitement palpable. He bent over the table and said, "Agni, I've been in the Crescent office since morning. I found out something rather interesting which could have a significant bearing on the case. I'm surprised Vaishali didn't mention this when we spoke to her yesterday."

"What is it?" Agni bent forward.

"Agni, there was a committee set up in Crescent a couple of months back."

"What kind of a committee?" the new revelation caught Agni's attention immediately.

"A committee investigating into allegations of sexual harassment that Sheetal had brought against Mr Mittal."

"You mean, Mr Vikrant Mittal?" Agni's eyebrows were raised.

"Yes, Sheetal had accused him of molesting her after working hours in his office."

"And what came out of that investigation?"

"Sheetal could not present conclusive evidence before the committee," Arya sighed. "Also, some of her colleagues spoke about her own lifestyle before the committee, which did not help her cause. So nothing really came out of it. However, Mr Mittal's image in the company definitely took a beating. He had been eyeing a promotion this year. He missed it. A lot of people in the company feel the incident may have had something to do with the decision of the management."

Agni got up from his chair and paced up and down the room. He stopped in front of the window and looked outside and then said, almost in a whisper barely audible to Arya, "Why do you think Vaishali did not mention the sexual harassment investigation? Who was she trying to protect?"

Day 3
01:00 p.m.

"I always saw this coming. With due respect to her departed soul, Sheetal was living on the edge," Vikrant Mittal's deep baritone filled Agni's chamber as he thrust his frame back on his chair, his arms folded at the back of his head, his shirt sleeves revolting against his sculpted biceps.

Agni and Arya exchanged glances.

"You know what?" Vikrant went on, "You need stability in your personal life to be productive at work. And Sheetal's lifestyle was beginning to affect her work."

"And did you ever have a word or two with her? I am sure, Mr Mittal, with your years of experience and your countless achievements you are a great role model at the workplace and a highly respected mentor for everyone in your office."

Agni managed to sound respectful and flattering. Arya was almost sure Agni had not meant half of what he had said. He often wondered why Agni had never considered a career in acting.

The effect of that false adulation, however, was immediately visible. Vikrant bent forward and a complacent smile almost lighted up his face.

"I did talk to her. But you know what, Officer? She just won't listen! Most people don't accept constructive criticism. Everyone wants instant success without having to walk that extra mile – just like that!" He gestured with a snap of his fingers. "At the same time, they don't understand the value of discipline. There is absolutely no restraint, no self-control. And no dearth of temptations these days in our so-called liberal, globalized society with changing moral values. It's so easy to get carried away, isn't it? What do you say, Officer?"

Agni looked up from his steaming cup of black coffee and looked Vikrant in his eyes. "Are you hinting specifically at Ms Sheetal, Mr Mittal?"

Vikrant became visibly alert. He threw his frame back in the chair once again, licked his parched lips with the tip of his tongue and remarked, "I did not mean anyone in particular. It was a general comment about the decadence in our society." He licked his lips again.

Arya gestured to a constable to get Vikrant a glass of water. Vikrant was sweating profusely inside the poorly ventilated room.

"I realize that. But you did mention a while back that Ms Sheetal had been living on the edge and that you had foreseen her tragic end?" Agni was in no mood to change the topic.

"That wasn't my personal opinion. That was common knowledge. It was fairly easy to see. Sheetal was never too discreet about her... let's say, adventurous lifestyle."

"Mr Mittal, are you aware if anyone in the office was involved with her?"

Vikrant struggled for words for a few seconds and then said, "None that I am personally aware of. She and I were not close enough for her to discuss her personal life with me."

"Who was she close to in the office, Mr Mittal?"

"I guess Vaishali knew her from college. Had seen the two of them hang around on a few occasions."

"Did you notice if the two of them were together in the party that evening as well?"

"I did see them together a few times. But then, as you will understand, one gets busy in one's own way in a party."

"Of course, I do realize that. Did you see her husband in the party that evening?"

"Was he there too? I don't think families had been invited!" Vikrant looked surprised.

Arya wondered if he was genuinely unaware of Sheetal's husband's brief presence in the party, or if he just feigned ignorance.

"He was there for a while...according to some of your colleagues we have spoken to."

"I never noticed him."

"Apparently they had a spat."

"They did?" Vikrant smiled condescendingly. "Isn't that what they did all the time anyway?"

Agni bent forward immediately and looked straight into Vikrant's eyes. "You seem to have a ring-side view of Ms Sheetal's marital discords, Mr. Mittal. I thought you said she never discussed her personal life with you."

Vikrant turned pale. His shirt had sweat patches. He undid the topmost button of his shirt and took a large gulp from the glass of water that had been placed in front of him sometime back. Taking his eyes off Agni's piercing gaze, he muttered in self-defence, "Again, Officer, that was not my personal opinion. The state of her marriage was known quite well to pretty much everyone."

"It seems to me from your statement, Mr Mittal, that the entire office took keen interest in Sheetal Mehra's private life. If I may call it private at all." Agni leant back against his chair and said, "I sincerely hope you have other more productive means of engaging what I assume is a highly paid workforce. Coming back to the topic of that fateful party, when did *you* leave the hotel that night, Mr Mittal?"

"I left around ten and was later called back to the hotel by the police. Quite a scandal! Doesn't do a company's reputation any good!"

"Talking of scandals," Agni bent forward once again and looked straight into Vikrant's eyes, "Is it true that there was a disciplinary committee set up some time back to look into allegations of sexual harassment that Ms Sheetal had brought against you?"

For a moment it seemed as if all movement, all sound in the room had been frozen. Vikrant had clearly not seen it coming. And then he mumbled, "Where did you hear about *that*?"

Like a seasoned hunter relishing the sight of the death throes of his prey, Agni reclined on his chair and smiled. "Like everything else about Ms Sheetal, let's assume for the moment that this was quite *well known to everyone in the office*, as well. It's true then?"

"Well... it's true," Vikrant drained the glass with one swig. "And I'm sure you also know that the committee found nothing against me. I have no idea why she brought those charges against me in the first place! In fact, she was the one who had been dropping hints all the time. I did not indulge as I knew that she was being used as a scapegoat by my rivals in the office who wanted to destroy me. It was a conspiracy against me by some of my peers. But it didn't work out. The committee declared that it had been an error of judgment on her part and warned her to be more cautious in future before her actions unduly tarnished the image of a respected leader of the company. Those were the exact words they used – *respected leader of the company!*"

Vikrant thumped on the wooden table top with his right hand as he emphasised on that phrase.

Arya thought if Vikrant Mittal was a liar, he was doing a pretty good job of it.

"The committee was quite lenient, I must say. I know of instances where the complainants were penalized heavily as they had not been able to prove their allegations," Agni commented.

"Exactly. The committee was rather merciful." Agni did not miss Vikrant's tone. He sounded almost regretful.

"And you? Were you equally forgiving towards Ms Sheetal?" That piercing look was back in Agni's eyes.

Vikrant had his shield up once again. "How does that matter? She is no more."

"You didn't answer me, Mr Mittal. Were you equally forgiving towards Ms Sheetal who had soiled your reputation in the office through what was proved to be a false allegation of sexual harassment?"

Vikrant kept looking intently at the table top. When he looked up, the hatred in his eyes was unmistakable. "Matters like that don't remain confined just within the four walls of the office, Officer. The investigation messed up my personal life. Some wounds never heal."

He paused again and then said, "But as I said, it really doesn't matter anymore. She is gone."

"Maybe it doesn't matter anymore *only because* she's gone," Agni smiled wryly as he reclined on his chair.

"What do you mean?" The colour had vanished from Vikrant's face.

"Did she ever hint about going to the media or to women's rights organizations with her allegations, the investigations in the company having obviously given *you* a clean chit?"

Vikrant muttered a feeble "No".

"What matters here, Mr Mittal, is the sequence of events leading to the death of one of *your* employees during *your* party." Agni paused, his eyes all over Mr Mittal's pallid countenance, "And such events invariably have their roots in the past – a past where an allegation by the victim had almost finished off *your* career and probably had repercussions in *your* personal life as well. And one can never tell what her plans had been for the future, the verdict of the committee having not been in her favour. Even if she had not explicitly hinted at seeking assistance from external agencies, had it not crossed your mind even for once that she might have been considering such a course of action?"

Arya noticed that Vikrant's fingers had started shaking. His shirt was drenched in sweat and his breathing was laboured. Sitting outside Vikrant's line of sight, he silently gestured to Agni.

Agni decided to stop the interrogation for the time being. "You may leave now, Mr Mittal. Revisiting the past is never quite easy, is it?" Finishing his coffee, Agni stood up.

When Vikrant Mittal stood up and turned to leave, Agni said, "And by the way, Mr Mittal, I don't think the committee had any reason to be lenient towards Ms Sheetal. I guess each one of you got the benefit of the doubt. There probably was not enough evidence to believe her," Agni paused. He then looked Vikrant Mittal in the eyes and said, "Maybe not enough to disbelieve her, either."

Day 3
04:00 p.m.

A gni had Sheetal Mehra's autopsy report open in front of him when Arya walked in. His legs were stretched out under his desk, the chair was pushed all the way back to the wall behind him. His eyes were on the report, latching on to every word, his eyebrows wrinkled.

He looked up from the report and asked, "What have you got, Arya? I bet you have been scraping the carpets of the Central Plaza hotel and sniffing around every dustbin and giving sleepless nights to the security and administrative staff there with your relentless questioning."

Arya smiled and said, "Those are the places, Agni, where I find evidences that prove the theories *you* form by screwing the minds of your suspects."

"It's called Psychological Analysis, Arya. You need to be slightly more respectful towards my art."

"Art indeed, Agni!" Arya did not try to stifle his bout of laughter. "The list of casualties from brain explosions in this very room would have been endless, had I not intervened at the right time on most occasions. Think of Vikrant Mittal a few hours back."

"Brain explosions! Where do you even find these words? And, by the way, are we going to spend the afternoon discussing your insightful critique of my interrogation techniques, or do you have anything remotely useful to report to me?" Agni sat up straight. He picked up the coffee mug that had long been emptied and put it back on the table with an indignant thud.

Arya pulled a chair for himself. "We've made progress in fact, Agni. I verified the times when each of the employees we had spoken to, had said he or she had left the party that evening. I checked registration numbers of the vehicles in the parking records of the hotel. The timings of vehicle movements tally fairly close with what we have in our recorded statements," Arya paused briefly. "Abhinav Mehra, of course, had arrived in a taxi from the airport which had been parked outside the hotel and I guess we cannot track the timing of his movements."

Agni was bent over the table, his eyes closed.

He exclaimed, "That doesn't help his case! What else do we have from the hotel records?"

Arya went on, "I also looked at CCTV footages from the hotel lobby and could identify at least Vikrant and Vaishali leaving individually at times that tally with what they had mentioned in their respective statements."

"What about the rest?" Agni asked.

"Most of the others walked out in groups from the party, or it is difficult to single them out in the CCTV pictures of guests moving into or out of the hotel. But we can do a more detailed study of the footages if we want to."

"Is there any other way someone can move into or out of the hotel?" Agni asked.

"Well...I happened to study the plan of the building, Agni, and realized that, the corridor adjacent to the restrooms ends in an emergency exit door that leads to a staircase which goes down to the parking lot at the basement. So it's perfectly possible for anyone to move out of that building without being seen by anyone in the vicinity of the discotheque or without having to cross the lobby area for that matter. However, that door usually remains locked, as I found out from the security staff. *Usually.*" Arya doodled on a piece of paper to explain the floor plan.

Agni got up from his chair and walked up and down the room, his arms folded behind him, his head lowered, wrinkles on his forehead. "I see. So it's perfectly possible for someone to escape the CCTV cameras in the lobby area if the emergency exit door leading to the staircase is left open for some reason, or because of plain oversight."

"You are right, Agni. I checked with the security staff, and some of them did say, off the record, that such a possibility could not be entirely ruled out."

"I can understand. Anything else?"

"That's all I have for now, Agni."

"Those indeed are interesting findings, Arya. You did a good job of snooping around, as usual."

"I will take that as a compliment." Arya smiled. "What do we have in the autopsy report?"

Agni walked up to his desk, picked up the file and handed it over to Arya.

The time of Sheetal Mehra's death was reported as between nine and eleven in the night. She had been strangled to death. Evidence of strangulation had been detected around her neck. She had apparently consumed a significant amount of alcohol.

There were traces of semen on her hands and shoes, but not around her genitals, suggesting indulgence in sexual activities with a male that did not end in intercourse. While looking for sexual assault evidence, as was warranted by the circumstances in which the body was discovered, there was no injury detected in her genitals. The pathologist who had conducted the autopsy had looked for signs of rape but had found none.

Unlike most of his peers in the force, Agni usually insisted on engaging a DNA laboratory in his investigations, if the circumstances so demanded. However, Agni was aware of the backlog of pending cases with the DNA laboratories, and did not expect a report anytime soon.

Also, over the years, he had come to accept the challenges of following such a procedure. He clearly remembered the court verdict in a murder investigation the previous year where DNA based evidence had been rejected on grounds of potential anomalies and high probability of false positives. Agni knew it had not been just the dated technology. In that particular case, the defence counsel had cited instances of inadequate sterility, not enough preservatives and callous handling of samples. No wonder then that the court had ruled out the DNA based evidence.

And then, in other cases, there had been hurdles like Right to Privacy and Right against Self-Incrimination acts which required the accused to consent to DNA tests. What further compounded the problem in India was the lack of a national database of DNA records.

Yet, in this particular case too, he had asked the laboratory to carry out more elaborate sexual assault tests on Sheetal's body. A swab for DNA samples around her breasts and genitals. DNA profiling of hair samples that might have been detected on her body or mingled with her own hair. DNA profiling of any skin cells that might have been detected under her nails in case she had resisted a sexual assault or murder attempt by scratching the arms or other body parts of the assailant.

Even if there had not been a rape, some of these evidences might reveal that she had consensually engaged in sexual activities, which might help provide vital clues.

Arya smiled and looked up at Agni, "DNA profiling? Again? You never give up, do you?"

Day 3
05:00 p.m.

Agni stopped in front of the magnetic board that hung on the wall right behind his desk, his arms folded behind him, his eyebrows wrinkled. The coffee mug on the table had been re-filled. A cup had also been placed before Arya who had the copy of the post-mortem report on the table in front of him.

Arya was all too familiar with Agni's ways. Right now in his mind, Agni was summarizing everything he had heard, noticed and inferred over the last few days.

Agni turned to Arya and picked up his coffee mug. "Let's crystallize what we have learnt so far and agree on the leads we need to follow. You have some time now, Arya?"

"Sure, Agni." Arya had been expecting this.

"Let's re-construct the events of that evening, shall we?" Agni took a sip from the mug.

"We have Sheetal Mehra – attractive, adventurous and trapped in a marriage gone sour. She goes around meeting men in the hope of finding someone she can get into a steady relationship with after breaking her marriage and doesn't mind kissing every frog that comes her way before one turns into her prince charming. She is probably involved with one or more of her colleagues, but even her close friend in the office doesn't know their names.

"On the night of the incident, she gets drunk, cozies up with men on the dance floor, which comes to the notice of her husband who drops in unexpectedly on his way home from a business tour. She refuses to leave the party, and they end up having a fight. The husband leaves, she gets herself a few more drinks at the bar and then heads for the toilet. Maybe alone, followed and then intruded upon. Maybe willingly with someone. A lot of them get their kicks from the risk of being 'caught in the act' in a public place, you know. With me, so far?" Agni checked.

Arya was bent over the desk, listening intently to Agni. He asked, "This person who accompanies her to the toilet with or without her knowledge – is this someone she knows?"

"Let's park that question for a while, Arya. That person maybe someone already known to her, maybe not. What matters is she eventually ends up with a man in the stall. She gets partially undressed, the two probably make out, and then she gets strangled to death. Mind you, there is no sign of rape. We don't know if her partner had murder in his mind when they stepped into the toilet, or if something happened in course of their rendezvous. Those are the questions we need to answer, Arya."

Agni paused for a moment and continued, "She dies, remains undetected in the furthest stall in the row for a while, before a woman in the housekeeping staff finds her. The party has all but ended and a lot of people have already left the hotel including, possibly, our murderer."

"And we end up in a situation where there's practically no witness to the crime."

"Yes. Let's now come to the question of who that person could be. Let's figure out what options present themselves before us. You go first."

Arya started with the obvious, "The assailant could have been a stranger not connected to Crescent at all, not known to Sheetal previously. He could be someone in the hotel who had just followed an intoxicated attractive woman to the hotel toilet and committed the heinous act."

Agni smirked, "In other words, the proverbial *needle in the haystack*. Also, there would possibly be some signs of struggle in such an event. What are the more *specific* options?"

Arya thought for a moment and said, "It could be someone in the office who had been in a relationship with Sheetal and had been dumped by her, like several others in the past. Sheetal had indeed been living on the edge, as we all know. But then, no one, not even her best friend at work, knows who among her colleagues she had been dating."

"Possible – and who else?"

"It could be someone we know and have spoken to."

"Exactly! Those would be the easiest to reflect upon, if, of course, we spend a little time analysing the statements of the individuals we have spoken to. Let's see what we've got here." Agni took a long swig of his coffee, as if in preparation for the analysis he had just embarked upon.

Agni walked excitedly up to the magnetic white board and picked up a marker pen.

Arya noticed Agni had already put down a few names there with notes, almost undecipherable to the lesser mortal, next to those names.

Agni circled the name of Abhinav Mehra.

"The husband. There is almost a fairy-tale flavour to this romance, what do you say?"

Agni looked at Arya.

"I guess so, Agni. But fairy tales never come true," Arya sounded philosophical.

"You are quite right, even with your inexperience in matters of the heart," Agni paused and then checked. "Or has there been any development in recent times that I am not aware of?"

"No one, Agni. I'm yet to—"

"I get it," Agni did not let Arya finish. This was no time to discuss Arya's uneventful love life.

"The marriage is on the rocks. The wife goes around meeting random men, looking for that one man with whom she can start life afresh. The husband lives in self-denial. He is still hopeful that he can turn things around. On his way home from a long business tour, he drops in at the party to pick his wife up. To spend an evening together after months of tension. Maybe go for dinner somewhere. See, he *is* trying, isn't he?"

"I feel the same way, Agni. In fact, when we spoke to him, he almost seemed to justify the wanton ways of his wife by blaming it all on his own work habits!"

"Yes. He did go to the extent of blaming himself for *the tragic outcome of his marriage* – there, I used his own words. But—" Agni paused dramatically as he paced up and down in front of the board, twiddling with the marker between his fingers.

"But let's consider how he must have felt in the party that evening. What does he see there? He sees his drunken wife cozying up with her male colleagues on the dance floor. He wants to take her back home and she refuses. She chooses to stay in the party. In fact, she tells him that she may be late. He may have imagined all kinds of reasons for her staying back. He gets livid. It's one thing to be suspicious, and something quite different to be a witness to the wayward ways of a spouse. He had never felt *more angry and more humiliated* all his life – there you go, his own words again."

Arya had always been in awe of the way Agni managed to commit specific lines from the statements of suspects to his memory and then use them at the right time in the right context. "I'm with you," he confirmed.

"They have a fight and he leaves the hotel around eight. Now, no one sees him leave. In fact, a lot of the guests didn't even notice him coming in. And, how do your findings tally with this?" Agni checked again with Arya.

"In truth, there is no evidence, Agni. And Abhinav has no alibi. He claims in his statement that he took a taxi from the airport that evening. The taxi was parked outside the hotel. There is no way to verify at what times he arrived at the hotel and left."

"You are right, Arya. What if he doesn't leave the hotel at around eight, as he claims? Remember here is a man who is seething in anger. Remember also that he can be remarkably in control of his emotions. So he won't make a scene in public even when his anger gets the better of him. We had more than a glimpse of that part of him in this very room the other day, didn't we?"

Arya picked up the cue from Agni and continued, "Maybe he follows his wife unnoticed to the toilet, gets into the stall along with the heavily drunk woman, bolts themselves in, undresses her without much of a resistance, gets into the act out of his sense of deprivation and frustration fuelled further by the events of the evening, and eventually ends up strangling her to death."

"Fantastic!" Agni stopped in his tracks and thumped the table in appreciation. "And when we bring up his motive and the lack of an alibi during the questioning, he almost throws a fit; his composure goes for a toss. Now you know why I said I place him pretty close to the top of my list of suspects."

"Let us now move on and look at the other players in this rather intriguing game," Agni walked back to the white board. He picked up the marker and drew a circle, this time around the name of Vikrant Mittal.

"Let's look at Vikrant Mittal."

Arya quipped, "He tried his best to wriggle out of the questioning on the night of the crime, tried to appear indifferent mentioning a meeting with his client the next morning, and your questioning here in this room turned him white and he almost had a stroke."

"Which, by the way, did not help him." Agni was quick to respond. "He has apparently been a successful professional through the years. He loves to look upon himself as a great role model that his team should emulate. However, we know of at least one skeleton the man has in his cupboard next to all his trophies. Sheetal Mehra accused him of having molested her in the office. A committee was set up, they found nothing and he was given a clean chit. That committee, however, did not have enough evidence to punish the complainant and let her go as well with a warning. We do not know for sure if that allegation was indeed false. But did Vikrant forgive her? I don't think he did. What do you think, Arya?" Agni smiled at Arya.

"I didn't think so during the questioning either, Agni. He hates that woman." Arya reclined self-assuredly on his chair.

"And I don't blame him. We know for sure that the investigation soiled his reputation in the office. It may even have had an impact on his professional growth in the company, as you found out from your questioning in the office. And we don't even know what it did to his personal life."

"He did hint during the questioning at an unfavourable impact the incident had on his private life." Arya remembered Vikrant Mittal's statement recorded in that room.

"Indeed. And one can never predict the influence of alcohol on an infuriated mind. Picture him in the party that evening, quite drunk himself, watching an intoxicated Sheetal Mehra on the dance floor with her male colleagues," Agni paused to take a sip from his cup and then continued. "This is the same woman who damaged his prospects in the company and probably, ruined his personal life – we do not know to what extent – with allegations of sexual harassment, which, she could not prove when called upon to do so. The man is also aware that she might go to the media or to one of the women's rights organizations with her story, since the investigations within the company did not end favourably for her. Is it too difficult to imagine, Arya, that he flies off the handle, follows her to the restroom unseen, in a fit of rage with revenge in his mind, forces his way into that stall, tries to have his way with her just as she had alleged, and exacts his revenge on the woman by throttling her neck? You can't deny the fact that he looks very strong physically."

"I see that highly probable too, Agni."

"Remember that he left the party around ten. He told us so himself and you verified his statement. So, in reality, he was in the hotel when the murder took place. And we also have a strong motive there."

"So that's our second lead?" confirmed Arya.

"Yes...we need to keep an eye on his movements."

Agni went back to the board and circled the name of Vaishali Arora. Arya said, "Wait a minute, Agni. Doesn't the autopsy report suggest that Sheetal Mehra was in the restroom with a man?"

"It does," Agni said. "Also, you did see Vaishali Arora in the CCTV footage leaving the hotel at the time she had mentioned in her statement. However, there are two reasons why I can't get her out of my mind. Firstly, why did she not mention the harassment investigation against Vikrant Mittal in her statement? Whose reputation was she trying to protect? Certainly not Sheetal's, as she mentioned her troubled marriage and her wayward ways herself. And secondly, I have a strong feeling she is not particularly happy about the fact that Abhinav Mehra married someone else and not her. In fact, I have a strong suspicion that she harbours special feelings for him. Abhinav Mehra also seemed to underplay his friendship with Vaishali during the interrogation."

Arya thought silently for a few minutes and said, "Even though she was not at the crime scene in person, she might have been an instigator, or even an accomplice. She might have created favourable circumstances for someone else to commit the crime."

"Exactly!" Appreciative thumping of the desk again.

Agni finally returned to his seat and reclined. With his eyes closed and fingertips brought together in an arch near his chin, he said, "And we didn't even look at the needles in the haystack, remember?"

Early July, 2015

New Town, Kolkata

Getting behind the wheel, I turned on the heating and got my car off the road as the rain lashed against the windows and the water ran down the glasses.

Meenakshi was next to me, the aroma of her wet body filled the air inside the car. "I can't thank you enough, ya. I was freezing out there on the road, getting soaked in these rains. The car couldn't find a better time to break down!"

Meenakshi went on, "For all you know, a car might even have knocked me down! You can barely see anything at an arm's length in these rains and people drive recklessly down this road. I have no idea, though, how long we may have to wait. You know what? Honestly, I don't have a lot of faith in the punctuality of these mechanics. Let me call them up one more time."

As she spoke on the phone, my eyes were all over her. The water dripped from her wet hair down her neck and trickled down below her shirt collar into the mysteries of her body. The white shirt was wet and clung to her skin. The cups of her fuschia pink bra formed an alluring contrast. She reclined on the seat, her toned thighs crossed, the outline of her hip and her thighs forming an alluring curve. I could feel the fire surging through my veins.

I had not noticed when she had stopped speaking on the phone.

"Hey," I looked up when I heard her speak again, "this is not the first time I have caught you staring." Meenakshi's eyes looked straight into mine.

She straightened her back, her breasts strained on the thin wet fabric of her shirt. "What did you have in mind when you offered to warm me up inside your car, haan?" She smiled mischievously, raising herself and bringing her face very close to mine.

Our eyes were fixed on each other. I could almost hear the drumming of our hearts. The only other sounds were the raindrops on the roof and the hum of the car heater.

"I like a man who keeps his promise." She demanded, "Warm me up."

Our lips met. She gave way to my probing tongue and it slid inside her warm gooey mouth.

Her breasts were pressed on my chest. I opened a couple of more buttons of her shirt and slid my hand in. Her skin was surprisingly warm and my fingertips on her deep moist cleavage seemed to send shock waves through her body. As our tongues caressed each other, she moaned into my open mouth. My hand instinctively moved along her belly, then her waist, dropping to her thigh. She uncrossed her legs and my hand glided higher. Her grip on my hair tightened and she let out a loud lustful moan when I felt her over her rain-soaked trousers.

Our trance was broken by the ring of her mobile phone. The tune of 'Careless Whispers' reverberated in the closed confines of the car. The phone was on the dashboard. I reached for it and *as I handed it over to her, I could see the picture of the caller. A balding man in black shades and a broad smile, the word 'Hubby' flashing on the screen.*

Meenakshi sat up and gestured to me with a finger on her lips. I could only hear her side of the conversation.

"Hey baby, are you home already?"

"Guess what? My car has broken down!"

"Yeah…I have already called them. They should be here any minute."

"No darling. You really don't have to come pick me up. Get some sleep. I know that was an awfully long flight!"

"I will be fine, sweetheart. The fact is that I left early so I could be home before you reached. I am so upset now!"

"Yeah…I'm waiting in the car. It's raining so hard!"

"Hmm…I so wish we could be together now."

"Shut up! Stop being naughty!"

"I will see you in a bit. Love you!"

She kissed into the phone before ending the call.

"That was my hubby, in case you haven't guessed. Such a spoil-sport!" Meenakshi tossed the phone back to the dashboard and grabbing the back of my head, pulled me closer and thrust her tongue inside my mouth, rubbing her breasts on my chest.

I did not feel anything but the familiar throbbing in my temples, as a tormenting crowd of faces flashed before my eyes.

The voices in my mind got louder with every passing minute…

Day 12
10:00 a.m.

"And what makes you think I can help?" Agni asked with a smile.

Inspector Vishwajeet Sinha said matter-of-factly, "Because this one is right up your alley, Agni. It's one of those cases that has left us clueless. You specialize in those, don't you?"

"And is this an official request? I ask because the murder has been committed in an area that's not under my jurisdiction."

"I can get the approvals for getting you involved. Agni, I could seriously do with some help here. Arya tells me the two of you are investigating a similar incident."

"We are investigating the murder of a woman who worked at one of the Information Technology companies in the New Town area. She was found dead in the toilet of the Central Plaza hotel in Park Street during an office party. But Vishwa, I will need to know more about the case *you* are handling to figure out if these two incidents are indeed similar."

Vishwajeet realized he had managed to get Agni interested. Agni was obviously fishing for more information. That was a good sign. Vishwajeet knew from experience – that was more than half the battle won.

Vishwajeet straightened his back, took a sip from the very sweet cardamom tea that had been served, and started, "The victim is a lady called Meenakshi Menon. She was in her thirties, married, no kids. She was the Director of Information Systems at Altius Finance. Her body was discovered by the side of the road that goes to the city from her office in Tech Park in New Town. This happened three nights back."

Agni asked, "Who found the body?"

"A couple of automobile technicians found her. It had been raining heavily since the evening. Her car had apparently broken down on that road and she had called up the on-road service from her mobile phone. The technicians in that area had been busy and had taken longer than usual to turn up. When they had started for the spot, they had tried her number a few times, but had not received a response. Thinking something had gone wrong with her phone, they had continued on their way. When they eventually arrived at the spot, they found her car parked off the road, but there was no trace of the lady who had called them.

"The road slopes down to a ditch. The ditch was overflowing that evening, and one of them spotted a body huddled up in the thick undergrowth at the bottom of the slope. They called the police immediately."

"And what makes you think it was not one or both of them that did her in?" Agni challenged Vishwajeet.

"We did explore that possibility. We checked their assignment logs and got in touch with the gentleman they said they had been working for before arriving at the spot. The timings matched. We also made a rough calculation of the time they would have taken to reach the spot from their last job and it all added up. Also, had these mechanics been involved, she would certainly have resisted and there would have been signs of struggle on the body. And possibly on them. There wasn't any."

"Okay. So these technicians reached the spot, they saw a body down by the ditch and like good Samaritans, they called the police. What did the police see when they reached the spot?"

"The technicians were there when the police reached. Meenakshi Menon was in her undergarments. Her mobile phone was discovered a few feet from her body – buried in the mud, as dead as its owner."

Agni smiled at the metaphor. "Ah! I absolutely adore your poetic streak, Vishwa. But let's not digress. What else did you see at the crime scene?"

Vishwajeet went on, "It had been raining for hours and we could hardly find significant clues at the crime scene. No marks of shoes, car tyres, fingerprints – nothing. Someone had probably strangled her and pushed her lifeless body down the slope to the ditch. As you know Agni, that area is in the outskirts of the city. The only traffic in the evening is from the office complex in the direction of the city. And it is not the best of roads to drive on in the rains after dark. Traffic had expectedly been sparse that evening. There was no witness."

"You mentioned the cause of her death was strangulation?" Agni wanted to confirm.

"Yes, Agni. That's how she died."

"What did you find inside the car?" Agni had wrinkles in his brow. One more of those cases where there was hardly any material evidence to go by. "Arya would not have liked this," he thought to himself, amused.

Vishwajeet replied, "Her purse was inside the car. In fact, it was the picture in her driver's license that helped us identify her. She was also identified later by her husband."

Agni asked again, "You said she was in her undergarments. Did you find her clothes at the spot?"

"We are yet to find her clothes."

"Was she raped or sexually assaulted in any way? What does the autopsy report say?"

Vishwajeet produced the report. "I have the autopsy report here with me, Agni. You can go through it. She died from strangulation. There were marks around her neck. The time of death is reported as between seven and nine in the evening. She was on her way home from work."

Agni picked up the report.

Vishwajeet continued, "No signs of rape but there were a few marks in certain parts of her body – neck, breasts, thighs. Those findings, coupled with the fact that she was in a state of partial undress, point towards sexual activities before death."

"Tell me about her husband. I am assuming you have already spoken to him."

"We did. He was on a business tour and returned the same evening. He went home straight from the airport. His chauffeur had picked him up. He was home at the time the murder was committed. They have a domestic help who has confirmed his statement. I also got his movements validated by the security guard of the apartment complex where he lives."

Agni bent forward and asked, "How did the husband react to the news, Vishwa?"

"The husband was devastated. Apparently, he had offered to drive down to the spot and pick her up when he had come to know that her car had broken down in the middle of nowhere and that she had been waiting for the technicians to turn up. But she had refused. He had been flying several hours from the United States and she had wanted him to get some sleep. He had obeyed, only to be woken up a few hours later with a nerve-racking call from the police to identify her body." Agni loved the way Vishwa always dramatized his accounts.

"Ghastly!" Agni whispered. He was lost in thought for a few seconds. He then muttered almost inaudibly, "But why did the wife refuse to be picked up by the good husband when she was stranded in the middle of nowhere in a car that had broken down, with none of the technicians in sight? To let him have an evening nap? That's one genuinely considerate wife, I must admit."

He looked up at Vishwajeet again and asked, "What else have we got as leads?"

"We went through Meenakshi Menon's call records. But we didn't have a lot of luck there as well. The last couple of calls had been made to the on-road service team of the car company, and she had received a call from her husband. The other calls over the rest of the day had been to her business contacts, which we have verified. And that's pretty much everything we have. Agni, if you are interested, I can secure a formal approval for your involvement in the investigations and share with you the reports of investigations so far, and everything else that you may need. But do you also see similarities with the case you are working on right now?"

Agni thrust his frame back on the chair and closed his eyes. After a while he spoke, "Indeed. The similarities are striking. In either case we have a woman, around her thirties, sexually violated, strangled and left to die. And in both cases, there is practically no witness and no significant evidence to go by. The circumstances, the times, the places seem to have been carefully chosen to ensure no witnesses." He opened his eyes, "Or, for all you know, the similarities may be coincidental. Meenakshi

Menon might have been killed by someone who had attacked her on that deserted road. The person might have tried to have his way with her, she must have resisted, and in the process, had been throttled to death and then left to die by the ditch. Perfectly possible. What do you think?"

"I don't rule out that possibility. But, as I told you Agni, it doesn't look like she had had to put up a fight in her final moments. So it's unlikely that this is the act of someone she did not know."

"You do have a point there," Agni sounded reflective.

Both men were silent for some time; Vishwa looking expectantly at Agni for him to come around, Agni reclining on his chair with his eyes closed and fingertips arched near his chin, weighing the pros and cons of ending up with a similar case on his plate.

After a few minutes, Agni stood up. "You know what? I am going to work on this one. Though I believe the clues to this mystery are not to be found on slippery roads and overflowing ditches. Meenakshi Menon, I'm quite sure, spent the greater part of her day in her office and that's where I'd like to start from. Who did you speak to there?"

"Her boss works from Delhi. She was the one in charge of her department here and didn't mingle a lot with the staff. So there wasn't much that the team could share with us other than work details that were known to everyone. She had a secretary – Priyanshi Basu. The girl is presently on sick leave. I was told she was not in a position to come down to the station. I had a brief conversation with her at her residence. Looks like she pretty much managed Meenakshi Menon's life for her. We should talk to her again to find out more about her deceased boss."

"We sure should," Agni said with a sense of finality and stood up. "Where does the girl stay? I would like to talk to her."

Day 13
11:00 a.m.

Priyanshi Basu looked beautiful even in her sickness.

Agni wondered it was a pity that only during the few weeks or months of homicide investigations he had the opportunity of meeting attractive women, but circumstances inevitably were never conducive to higher ambitions. There he was, single and brooding through his days and nights, and as he looked into the eyes of the woman an arm's length away from him, right across the low coffee table in her living room inside her Jodhpur Park residence, he could not push aside thoughts of how the warmth of a compassionate hand on his sore heart would feel. He was shocked as he realized he had not felt that way for another woman for quite some time.

"I understand this must have been a rude shock for you," Agni managed to start the conversation after several awkward minutes, during which he had been searching for the right words for an introduction. In the meantime, the maid had come and taken orders – a cup of tea for her, a black coffee without sugar for him.

She nodded.

"I'm sorry I have to speak to you while you are on a sick leave. But, as you can understand, we need to get down to business real quick."

She nodded again. Not a word spoken so far.

The tea and the coffee arrived.

She took a sip and then broke the silence finally. "I'm sorry I couldn't share a few details with your colleague when he spoke to me earlier. There are a few things I wasn't comfortable discussing with my parents around. They can be pretty conservative in some ways."

She was alone in the house that afternoon, with only her grandmother for company.

"I'm not even sure if I would go back to that office again," she paused briefly. "With Ma'am not around."

"I understand. Looks like she was much more than a boss to you?"

"She was. I was in desperate need of a job when I saw the advertisement for the position of personal secretary to one of the Directors of Altius Finance. I wanted to try my luck, though I knew I didn't have enough experience. Ma'am interviewed me. She spoke to me for about half an hour. And then she said she liked my honesty and my willingness to take up a challenging job even though I didn't have the number of years behind me." Tears welled up in her eyes.

Don't cry please, Agni prayed silently. He knew he was pathetic at handling a woman's tears.

She pulled herself together, thankfully. "And then she literally took me under her wing. She trusted me blindly. And I never gave her a reason to regret her decision. I hope so. May her soul forgive me if I sound immodest."

"I am sure you did a wonderful job," Agni reassured her.

"I know there were tongues that wagged in the office as you can imagine. People never figured out why Ma'am had appointed as her secretary someone who they felt was very young for the position. They also didn't like the fact that Ma'am entrusted almost her entire life to me."

"And now that she's no more, you don't want to go back to that office?" The empathy in Agni's voice was not lost on Priyanshi.

"You guessed it right. I am not even sure if they will have a job for me anymore." Priyanshi's cheeks were flushed. There was a sudden hint of dismay in her otherwise calm, sad eyes. "I'll need some more time to get over the shock. And then I'll look for a new job. I learnt so much working with Ma'am." Her eyes had tears again.

She looked around for a handkerchief. Agni wanted to pass his on, but he was not even sure if it was clean enough to be offered to a lady.

"Priyanshi, I was wondering if you would be able to tell me how Ms Menon's last day in office was."

"Well...nothing out of the ordinary, really. She would reach office around half past eight every day, get busy with her meetings, have lunch in her cabin, work till around seven and then leave. It was pretty much the same that day."

"And may I assume you are the one who managed the schedule of her meetings and her appointments?"

"I did. It was part of my job."

"And those were not always meetings with her colleagues in Altius Finance, right? In her position, I'm sure she met a lot of people from other organizations as well?"

"Of course. She worked with all of our vendors."

"Would you be able to share with me details of all the meetings she had had over the month before her death?"

"I will. I have her meeting details in my office laptop. It's with me."

"That would be a lot of help. I am curious about who she would usually meet with. Do you have any idea?"

"I can tell you. She was the Director of Information Systems. She looked into all the IT projects that ran in the company. She had a team of project managers in Altius Finance that she would meet regularly to check the status of all the work going on in the company. And then there were the vendors. Altius Finance engages a number of vendors for software development and maintenance and also for supplying the hardware for running all those systems. We issue tenders for such projects. She used to manage all those bids. She would meet with those vendors, along with her colleagues from our Purchasing division, to finalize such deals. Her calendar would be unbelievably busy every working day of the year."

"I can imagine. Did she have a life outside work?"

"Of course she did! I thought she was great when it came to time management. There was so much to learn from her."

"All of that sounds wonderful," Agni bent forward as if to lend his ears to a secret. "What is it then that you wanted to discuss in private, something you feared your parents might not approve of?"

Priyanshi looked hesitant. For a moment she regretted having made that statement in the first place. What she had planned to say was perhaps immaterial. The very next moment she wondered, what if it had anything to do with the murder? She would never be able to forgive herself if she did not open up before the police and if that stood in the way of identifying the murderer.

"There was gossip in the office about her."

"What kind of gossip?" Agni's eyes narrowed. He listened to Priyanshi intently, bent forward, his elbows resting on his thighs, fingertips arched on his chin.

"About the deals she approved when the tenders were issued." Priyanshi was suddenly cautious, choosing every word with the utmost care.

"Was it about money?" Agni asked the obvious.

Priyanshi was quiet for some time. Agni realized Priyanshi needed the time to put her thoughts together.

"Was it money?" Agni asked again.

"Not really," Priyanshi looked down, as if she herself had done something that she was not proud of. Agni could not but appreciate her loyalty and her intense feelings for her departed boss. She finally managed to speak. "There were rumours that she handed many of those bids to vendors who didn't really qualify."

"I do understand that. But why would she do that?"

"There were rumours that she would get involved physically with people from those companies and that would often influence her decisions." She blurted the words out.

That was a first for Agni. He had heard of men in positions of authority signing business contracts in exchange for sexual favours. He was even aware of so-called 'fixing agencies' that deal managers often engaged, which essentially were in the business of connecting decision makers in corporate houses with women. It was quite a revelation to see the roles reversed.

"You said she shared her life with you. You were her trusted secretary. If anyone knows if there was any truth in those rumours, it has got to be you," Agni was impatient to know the truth.

"I cannot tell you anything more." Her face was buried in her palms. Agni saw her shoulders shaking. "Ma'am will never forgive me for this," she muttered between her sobs.

"Priyanshi, your intentions are honest. You decided to share this with the police as you know pretty well that there could be a connection between her indiscretions and her tragic end. Would *you* be able to forgive yourself if the killer went free simply because you didn't come clean about this?"

"I don't know...I don't know. Oh god, help me!" Priyanshi broke down.

Priyanshi calmed down after a few minutes. She sniffed, wiped her face and said in a more resolute voice, "Yes. Those rumours were true. I made some of the hotel reservations and holiday bookings myself."

"And was Mr Menon aware?" Agni asked.

"I don't think so. Ma'am used to hint at *his* several affairs."

"Do you know about those for sure?"

"I have no idea."

There was a brief awkward silence between them before Priyanshi spoke again, "When I heard about her murder, a number of possibilities came to my mind. It could have been one of those bidders who had lost out on a deal as she had preferred someone else she had been intimate with. Or, it could have been someone she had been involved with but the deal had not worked out for some reason. I wanted to share this with the police as it could be any of those men. But I didn't want to talk about her personal life before my family as they have a lot of respect for my job and for Ma'am. Have I done the right thing?"

"You have, Priyanshi. There is nothing to worry about. Everything you have shared or will share with the police henceforth will be in strict confidence and will be used solely for the purpose of this investigation. As I mentioned earlier, I would like to see her calendar for the month before her death. And the list of vendors she had been talking to in her last days. Can you help me with that?"

"I will."

"You said you have the details in your office laptop at home?"

"Yes...you can pick up those details right away."

Agni waited in the living room as Priyanshi went to get the meeting records. The living room was tastefully done up. There were a couple of bookcases that reached halfway up the walls, stuffed mostly with fiction. Agni noticed a few paintings, framed on the walls. His eyes were drawn to a picture of a wide-eyed girl in plaits holding up a trophy. A younger Priyanshi, of course. Her face had not changed much over the years. Agni smiled at her moment of glory in her teens.

Priyanshi returned after a while with a pen-drive.

"I have copied her meeting schedule for the entire month. You can always call me up if you have more questions," Priyanshi said.

Agni thanked her profusely and left. Her smell seemed to linger in the air around him.

On his way back to his office, between flashes of Priyanshi's beautiful and vulnerable face, the similarities between the two cases kept haunting Agni's mind.

Vishwajeet and Arya were in Agni's office later that morning. Agni filled them in on everything he had heard from Priyanshi.

"Doesn't look like Meenakshi Menon had too many friends in the office, barring a few loyalists like Priyanshi," Arya remarked.

"You're probably right Arya," Agni said. "That's what I've been thinking as well. Apparently she kept to herself, didn't go around the floor, and there were rumours about her loose morals in the office, which, as Priyanshi mentioned to me, were indeed true. The question then is – how does this knowledge about her perception among her colleagues help us?"

Vishwajeet said, "Professional rivalry could have been the motive, Agni."

Agni replied, "I doubt, Vishwa. If we're talking about professional rivalry here, a colleague could easily benefit by finding out facts that proved her improprieties in the matter of awarding contracts and reporting to higher authorities. Someone might even have set her up and caught her in the act. That could finish her career. That could even put her marriage at risk. What better way to finish her? All that without a drop of bloodshed."

"And how about one of the vendors who had been dealt a wrong hand because of her unlawful behaviour?" Arya suggested.

Agni thought for a while. "Look at it this way, Arya. She was someone who had the authority to make procurement decisions. And she was someone who *could be manipulated*. Now which vendor wouldn't love someone like her? If I were one of those vendors and knew that she had been biased towards some of the others in the past, and I happened to know what 'made her tick', wouldn't I go out of my way and woo her, to get her on my side? Killing her out of vengeance would not solve my problem. For all you know, her successor could be someone *not malleable enough*. For a vendor, it always helps to have a corrupt decision maker in *power*, not dead in a ditch," Agni smiled.

Arya said, "So what you are suggesting is that in spite of her not being very popular inside and outside the office, no one would go to the extent of killing her for professional reasons."

"Exactly! There are personal issues involved here, as with the murder of Sheetal Mehra," Agni paused and looked at the other two, "though I don't rule out the possibility of such personal issues having their roots in the office."

"And that's the reason why you want to go through records of her meetings over the last few weeks to figure out who she might have met in connection with her work in the days before her murder?" Arya checked with Agni.

"It's great to see you catching up fast," Agni winked. "At the same time, we should keep looking for leads in the office. We *have* to find someone who can tell us more about how Meenakshi Menon went about her business."

Day 13
02:00 p.m.

Agni had barely walked back to his office after lunch when Arya stormed in. He was brimming with excitement.

"Looks like you have brought news, Arya." Agni stretched his hand in the direction of a chair, signalling Arya to take a seat. Arya was too excited to pay heed.

"Agni, you won't believe this! While I've been following up on the leads, I've also been checking for similar incidents in other parts of the city. It occurred to me when Inspector Vishwajeet Sinha reported an almost similar murder in the New Town area that we could check for similar incidents in other parts of the city over the last few months, and see if there was a pattern. Does that sound reasonable?"

Agni nodded, "It does, Arya. And I must say that's rather ingenious of you! And what have you got?"

"Agni, I now have information on another murder that happened two months back. It looks similar to both the cases we are dealing with here and no arrests have been made yet."

"Tell me more." Agni now sounded impatient, sitting on the edge of his desk, facing Arya.

"This one happened in May this year. The victim was a married woman in her mid-thirties. Husband works in the United States. She lived alone in the Salt Lake area. She was found in the house, strangled to death. The body was scantily clad but, as in the cases of the other two ladies we are dealing with, the autopsy didn't suggest rape." Arya paused for breath and reached for the glass of water on Agni's desk.

A cold wave ran down Agni's spine. There was more to these murders than met the eye.

"Arya, we have had three murders in the city in two months, two of them in less than three weeks. All of them follow a similar pattern and murders with patterns always make me fear the worst."

Agni looked grave and anxious. He walked across the room to the window looking at the overcast afternoon sky.

He muttered, "Three is not coincidence, Arya. There is definitely a threat looming large over this city."

Day 13
07:00 p.m.

*T*he strand of hair I had plucked off Meenakshi's head was now firmly glued to a page in my scrapbook. Like the rest of them. Those were my trophies. I closed my eyes as I remembered every word she had uttered, every move she had made, every lustful moan that had escaped her lips, and then every fruitless attempt she had made to hold on to dear life as my fingers around her neck had sunk in deeper. I remembered how her face had changed colours, from a warm red to a cold deathly white. I remembered how she had been a temptress one minute and a corpse the next, the look of unbelieving horror frozen for eternity in those dead eyes.

Her clothes were right there, on the bed in front of my eyes. I remembered how she had thrown them off herself. They still had her smell. Or was it my mind playing tricks with me?

I folded her clothes neatly and put them away with the scrap-book inside the cupboard. That cupboard – I called it my 'shrine'.

I poured myself a whisky and reclined on the sofa. I was getting better. The remorse had finally vanished completely. The *relief was overwhelming, though more and more short-lived with every execution. But who was I to complain? I was the one chosen by destiny to exterminate the scum of the society.*

There was another rumble in the sky. There had been one when Meenakshi had finally given up her fight in the car and her head had rolled to a side.

Meenakshi Menon, Director, Information Systems, Altius Finance – dead as a rag doll, stripped to her inners, kicked out of my car, rolling down the slope, landing somewhere by the ditch.

She had always reminded me of Anita. Anita was my very first supervisor. The year was 2007. The place was Bengaluru. I was twenty-three.

"You seem to be in a hurry to go back home. I thought you stay alone," Anita threw her stilettos off and walked towards the dining table to pour herself a glass of water. "Who do you want to go back to?" Her throaty laughter filled the almost dark room.

I had completed my graduation a year back and was in my first job. I had been working with Anita all along and she had always been a great boss to work with, the stories in the grapevine about her being a 'man eating tigress on the prowl' notwithstanding. She had never made indecent advances. But there was something about her demeanour that night that was making me uncomfortable.

The house where I lived as a paying guest with an old couple was a short walk away from her bungalow. Though I had started off alone after the office party that evening, she had stopped her car and had offered me a ride when she had chanced upon me at the bus stop. I was suddenly not sure if I had made the right decision coming along with her.

"Have a seat now and make yourself comfortable. It's way past office hours, so leave the formality at the door," Anita was now a curvaceous silhouette against the faint yellow light seeping through the thick lampshade.

I sat down awkwardly at the edge of the sofa. "There is... well...no one to go back to," I forced a smile and mumbled, "but...you know...the house doesn't have a separate entrance to my room. They go to bed early and don't like my returning too late."

Anita was now at less than an arm's length. She sat next to me, her face turned towards me.

"I'm sure you get away every time with that charming smile of yours, don't you?" she spoke almost in husky whispers.

As she raised her arms and ran her fingers through her hair, my eyes were drawn to her accentuated breasts. Her body filled out that purple dress that showed off her curves and had attracted the lusty gaze of all the men in the party all evening.

She finished the water, got up again and walked towards the bar.

"You don't mind having a couple more drinks, do you? Let's have a small private party – just the two of us," she looked back over her shoulder and winked at me, as she poured vodka into two glasses. The bar was closer to the lampstand and I could not take my eyes off her shapely back, the panty line cutting through, as she bent over the bar counter.

"Cheers to our first little house party. I am sure there will be many more to come," she whispered as our glasses clicked.

Anita was back on the sofa, dangerously close to me. The dress was up a few inches above her knees, showing off her immaculately waxed legs. I tried to start an office conversation awkwardly, trying hard to avoid looking at her deep cleavage with the locket buried between her breasts and the beads of sweat shining there in the dim light. I had no idea what was making me dizzy – the vodka after all the free drinks I had been gulping down all evening at the party or the smell of the woman in front of me. The room felt way too hot. The walls seemed to close in on me, even as I felt desire raging through my veins.

"Can we for god's sake do the office talk tomorrow morning?" Anita's fake rebuke shut me up.

She finished her glass in a flash and put it down on the low table in front of the sofa with a thump. In no time, her fingers were at the back of my head, running through my hair. I could feel her warm breath on my face.

"You must have heard a lot about me, I felt her warm lips planting impatient wet kisses all over my face. "Guess what? They are all true. Anita is a bad girl, and you know what? That takes a load off my chest. I don't really have a reputation at stake here."

The tip of her tongue made its way down my jaw, down the side of my neck and up again along my throat, her moist lips making a lingering halt around my Adam's Apple. Her lips sucked in mine, and her saliva trickled into my mouth as her vodka soaked tongue slid inside like a hungry snake. I felt the softness of her breasts, almost spilling out of that skimpy dress, on my chest even as the fever spread all over her body. Her deft fingers had already started unbuttoning my shirt.

My hands instinctively reached out and pulled her closer to me. I found the zip of her dress at the back and lowered it all the way down to the small of her back, my hands caressing her smooth bare back that now had a thin film of sweat, as I searched for the clasp of her bra.

She moaned in anticipation as I unhooked her bra and pulled the straps of her dress and her bra off her shoulders. In no time I was kissing her on her neck and her bare shoulders as she held me by my head and thrust her bare breasts at me.

I smelt her between her breasts, a heady cocktail of her perfume and her feminine aroma. Seductive moans escaped her mouth as she squirmed on the sofa.

I felt her nails digging into my back. She reached out for my glass of the vodka and gulped down whatever was left in it.

She pushed me away and threw herself back on the sofa, sinking in its soft depth. Her dress was now bunched around her waist. Her legs were spread – one reaching down to the furry carpet below and the other thrown over the sofa. Her body arched in invitation. My hands reached behind her and held her up by the waist.

That was when I hit something on the table and it landed on the carpet with a dull thud.

I turned my face away from Anita and looked at the source of the sound. It was a picture in a steel frame. A family picture of Anita with a man and a little girl standing between them with a big smile on her face. That must be her husband. He was obviously not home. And I knew the daughter had been sent to a boarding school a few months back.

That picture suddenly brought back memories. Memories that haunted me as nightmares and woke me up from my sleep night after night. Images raced through my mind, drawing fresh blood from the wound I have been carrying in my soul for a few years now.

I looked back at Anita, sprawled on the sofa with her eyes shut, sweating in the throes of passion. The air in the room felt thick with treachery and deceit. I felt for the man in the picture, just as I had felt for another man a few years back. And I felt used, all over again.

That face contorted with lust, that sweaty slithering body – everything about Anita at that moment reminded me of my stepmother. And of the night I would not forget for the rest of my life.

I was twenty and in Engineering college. I had come home for my winter holidays. It was the week before Christmas. As luck would have it, my father was on a business tour that could not wait and I was alone in the house with my stepmother.

She was unusually nice to me that whole day. But every time she ran her fingers through my hair or touched me on some pretext or the other, I felt uncomfortable.

That was a rather cold winter night, and I woke up with a start as I felt something warm and moist on my face. As I opened my eyes, I saw my stepmother next to me under my blanket, planting wanton kisses all over my face. I was shocked to discover she had nothing under her slip. Her smell filled the still air inside the blanket.

She remained unperturbed when she saw me open my eyes and inched closer to me. I felt a bare leg wrap around my waist. Taking my hand, she placed it on her thigh. Her skin felt warm and clammy.

I did not know how to end the farce. Dad's face flashed before my eyes – his hair more grey than black, the wrinkles beginning to show up around his eyes, always eager to please his new, much younger bride. She used to be a secretary in his office and rumour had it that they had been seeing each other even before mom had passed away a year back. At that moment, I remembered mom and tears streamed down my eyes.

My stepmother had by then thrown the blanket aside and licked and scratched her way down my body. When I looked *down through the blur of my tears, I could see her, face contorted with lust, desperately trying to get me up. She gave up after a while.*

"The men in this house are all the same," she shouted as she got off my bed. "Ever heard of hormones, Son?" she shouted as I saw her disappear outside my room.

"Have you already emptied your balls? That is, if you have them in the first place," I was brought back to my senses as Anita cried out. She sounded frustrated. She needed me badly that very moment.

And I was not going to let her use me. In her, I saw the same woman who had made the most of her husband's absence and crept under a blanket years back to devour a younger body. That woman had inflicted on my soul a wound that never healed. And as the pain from that wound took me in its vice-like grip, my animal instincts cowered off. I had not realized when I had gone limp.

"Shut up bitch!" I cried out. My voice echoed around the empty house as I buttoned up my shirt and buckled my belt. "And I don't care if I lose my job for this."

As I stormed out of the room after a while, I looked back one last time at the woman lying on the sofa. I did not know then that that image would haunt me for the rest of my life.

I started running and did not stop till I reached my house out of breath, my shirt drenched in sweat.

While it was common practice among the guys in office to bestow Don Juan status on whoever caught the fancy of Anita, I chose to keep my experience a secret.

I quit the job after a few months and returned to Kolkata.

Day 13
08:45 p.m.

Agni looked at his watch as he stood in front of the imposing compound wall. That was the time the Professor had said would be best for the meeting.

The roads in that part of Kolkata were empty at that time of the night, with the few odd private cars speeding up and down occasionally. Alipore was one of the few places in the city where one could still breathe in some fresh air. The Command Hospital of the Air Force was close. The Jail was not too far away either.

The watchman opened the gate with a smile and Agni walked down the gravelled path that went right through the impeccably maintained lawn up to the house of Professor Parikshit Roy. The trees that lined the compound wall looked like patches of dark ink against the night sky. There was a dog barking somewhere in the distance. That was pretty much the only sound that reached Agni's ears.

Professor Roy lived alone in that house. The sitting room was on the ground floor where the Professor met his visitors. There was also a library at the other end of the room. The bedrooms were upstairs.

Professor Roy was one of the eminent psychologists in the city. Agni had known him for several years now. In addition to his regular profession of clinical psychology and counselling, the Professor took keen interest in the subject of criminal psychology. And there had been several instances in the past when Agni had paid the learned Professor a visit or two to discuss particular cases where he had felt the intricate workings of the human mind had had a larger role to play than more commonplace motives. Agni would invariably return enlightened by the priceless insights of the Professor, who, in return, would have his vast repository of experiences further enriched.

When Agni walked in, the Professor was already in the sitting room, smoking his trademark cigar.

He stood up and extended his hand to Agni, "Welcome Agni. You are on time, as always!"

Agni shook hands with him and said, "Thanks Professor. When you manage to find an hour for me from your schedule, I better make good use of every available second." The two men laughed.

The Professor called out to an attendant who stayed with him. He returned after a while with their favourites – Cabernet Sauvignon for both of them, with cheddar cheese and some roasted cashew nuts. He was well aware of what the men loved to drink.

The two men sipped the wine in silence. The Professor was the first to speak.

"So, what is it this time?" He had a smile at the edge of his lips.

Agni took a bite of the cheese and a sip of the wine. "There have been three murders in the city over the last two months, Professor. The last two of them in less than three weeks. Who knows, there may have been more! I thought I would run this by you."

"And what's the pattern this time?"

"Married women in their thirties, all strangled to death. There are evidences of sexual activities before death, but, in each case, rape can be ruled out. One was killed in a toilet, another strangled and left to die by a ditch on the roadside. And the third woman had been killed in her house under similar circumstances. We know for sure that two of these women had multiple intimate relationships outside marriage. We are yet to find out about the other."

"There does seem to be a pattern. Do you have suspects?"

Agni explained his observations and inferences in the two cases so far.

"You seem to be making fairly good progress here," Professor Roy took a sip of the wine. "I especially like the way you have interpreted the statements and the behaviour of the people you have spoken to. But what you need to remember, Agni, is that the key to solving a case of this nature is to study the pattern. You need to examine every aspect of the pattern – the circumstances, the people involved, the timing, the places, the motives and, in some cases, the apparent lack of any motive. You know what I mean, right?"

"I do, Professor," Agni latched on to every word Professor Roy had to say, like the boy in the front bench of the class, mesmerized by a profound discourse from the lecturer.

Professor Roy paused for a while and took a drag of his cigar. Agni saw the glow at the tip of the cigar get brighter and then the smoke curled out of the Professor's mouth forming transient patterns around his face. Professor Roy continued, "When you have every aspect of every incident analysed, that's when the real challenge surfaces. You need to figure out what's common among those cases – those almost invisible threads that tie them together. Of course, you need to have the eyes to find those threads. And the threads will eventually lead you to the truth."

Agni thought for a while, assimilating what Professor Roy had just said, before he spoke again.

"So, in essence, instead of handling these cases as discrete, we need to figure out what's common among them."

"That's right Agni. Go figure out the links," the Professor smiled.

The two men remained silent for a while as they finished the wine. Agni glanced at his watch and stood up. Professor Roy lived a disciplined life and Agni was well aware that it was dinner time for the Professor.

"Thanks Professor for making the time and sharing your thoughts, and, as usual, the wine is great." Agni smiled.

They shook hands again and the professor said, "I will be very interested to know what comes out of your investigations, Agni. I am sure you will find the murderer. Don't forget to let me know when you do."

"I will, Professor. And I may have to come back again if matters get more complicated as the investigation progresses."

"You can visit me anytime, Agni. I always find your work fascinating and it gives me immense pleasure to be of any help whatsoever."

As Agni walked out of Professor Roy's house, there was an almost foreboding rumble in the dark overcast night sky. Agni wondered where the malefactor was lurking at that moment. Agni wondered what he would be up to next. He had no way of knowing.

As Agni stood in his balcony staring into the night, the breeze ruffling his hair, there was a storm in his mind under the apparent calm. He finished the single malt and went back to the study. Switching on his laptop, he plugged in the pen drive. Priyanshi had meticulously copied into the drive Meenakshi Menon's meeting schedule for the last month.

As Priyanshi had mentioned earlier in the morning, the meetings were either internal meetings with Meenakshi Menon's project teams at Altius Finance, or meetings with prospective vendors. Agni could recognize quite a few popular IT firms as he went through the list of vendors Altius Finance worked with.

And then he noticed it.

Just a few hours back, he had discussed with Professor Parikshit Roy links among the murders and there was one, right there in front of his eyes, on the laptop screen. Agni looked at his watch. It was close to two in the night, certainly not the appropriate time to call up a lady on sick leave. He would have to wait till daybreak.

In the two weeks preceding her death, Meenakshi Menon had met twice with Crescent Technologies.

Day 14
08:00 a.m.

Priyanshi took the call after a few rings. Agni had almost decided to end the call, unhappy over the fact that he would have to wait some more.

"Hello?" Priyanshi sounded tentative on the other side of the line.

"Hi, good morning. This is Agni."

"Good morning. Is everything okay?" When one is recovering from a shock, every phone call threatens to have brought bad news.

Agni tried to sound as reassuring as he could. "Everything is fine, Priyanshi. Don't worry."

"Thank God! I'm sorry…it has all been so unexpected, with every phone call I—"

Agni did not let her finish. "I perfectly understand, Priyanshi. I happened to go through Ms Meenakshi's meeting details last night. I must thank you for sharing all the information with me. They were extremely valuable."

"You are welcome. But I only did what *you* said would help the investigation."

"Of course. Now, coming to the reason why I called you – what I noticed in the records, Priyanshi, is that in the four weeks preceding her death, Ms Meenakshi had had two meetings with a company called Crescent Technologies. Do you happen to know anything about those meetings?"

The line went silent for a while. Priyanshi was probably trying to recollect the name of the company, Agni thought.

Then she spoke. "They develop software, right?" Priyanshi checked with Agni.

"Indeed. The meetings must have been in connection with some project Ms Meenakshi had been planning?"

"I remember now. Ma'am had had a few meetings with them recently in connection with a new project. There were some other vendors involved as well."

"That helps, Priyanshi. I know I am being very demanding here, but would it be possible for you to find out who from Crescent she had met with?"

"I can find that out for you. There is a Senior Manager in Ma'am's team who forwarded the meeting invitations to attendees from the different companies, after I had scheduled those meetings as per Ma'am's availability and blocked her calendar. I will check with him and let you know who from Crescent had met with Ma'am."

"That would be most helpful, Priyanshi. Can you call me back on this number as soon as you find out the name of the person from Crescent?"

"I will."

"Thanks Priyanshi. I will wait for your call." Agni hung up.

4 p.m., Same day

So, ACP Agni Mitra has now got involved in Meenakshi Menon's case. Is he really as good as the media makes him out to be? I have read and heard about some of his 'exploits', but then the media is notorious for inflating every little story to grab eyeballs.

The identical circumstances of the murders must have caught his attention. My signature style has not gone unnoticed. Is that something I should be proud of?

Then, what happens to the older cases? It may just be a matter of time before he starts poking his nose into those as well. I can feel his involvement suddenly shaking up the status quo. It is now important for me to follow these investigations more closely than ever before. From the selfish interest of protecting myself. And my cause. All this is for a cause, after all.

I also need to find out more about the detective. To figure out what makes him tick. And most importantly, to figure out if he really is good enough to pose any serious threat.

As I still have a lot to do.

Day 15
08:00 a.m.

Agni was in the shower getting ready for work. It took him a while to step out and receive the call. He glanced at the clock. Eight in the morning.

It was Arya.

"Hey Arya, what's up?"

"Agni, where are you?"

"I just about managed to step out of the shower to talk to you. Why?"

"You need to come down to Elliot Road. As soon as you can make it."

"Elliot Road? What's the matter?"

"I'm calling from the residence of Abhinav Mehra. He's dead. Hung himself from the fan in his living room with his wife's dupatta sometime last night." Arya paused for a moment. "Agni, come down as soon as you can, please. I'm waiting."

The address Agni had was that of a three-storied house. The house was at the end of a narrow lane off the main road. As he got off the car, Agni looked around himself. The lane was congested with traffic. Motorcycle and auto-rickshaw horns assaulted eardrums. People sat idly on the ledge of houses that lined both sides of the lane while some walked leisurely to neighbourhood stores right through the traffic to buy items of grocery, paying no heed to the bellowing horns. The road was muddy and slippery from rains all through the night before. The heat and the humidity were unbearable, even though it was just about nine in the morning.

A wall ran around the house. There was a gate through that wall, which opened to a narrow alley. Agni walked in through that iron gate which was presently open. To his left a few feet down that alley was another door that opened to a flight of stairs that led him to the Mehras' apartment on the second floor of the building. The Mehras were the only occupants of the second floor. There was another tenant on the first floor of the house and the owner, an old man in his seventies, lived in the ground floor with his son.

Arya met Agni at the entrance to the Mehras' flat.

"They had to break the door open," Arya explained as they walked into the apartment. In the living area, Agni saw the lifeless body of Abhinav Mehra hanging from the fan, a purple dupatta around his neck. The eyes protruding, the mouth gaping, hint of a tongue. Dishevelled hair, a high neck maroon T-shirt, ash-coloured tracks.

"No suicide note." Arya pre-empted Agni's question.

There was an overturned chair on the ground, its role in the tragedy evident. Agni looked around the room. No visible sign of a break in. Everything apparently in order. A few pictures of the couple in happier times around the room. In one of the pictures, Vaishali had her arms around the shoulders of her friends, both in wedding attire. Even from a distance, that smile looked forced.

Arya introduced Agni to some of the people who had gathered in the living room. Agni saw the landlord, his son who appeared to be in his thirties, and a lady who Arya mentioned lived in the first floor apartment. Her husband left for work pretty early every day. He had already left the house when the body was discovered.

"Who found the body?" Agni checked.

"The boy who delivers milk in the area," Arya looked in the direction of a boy in a half-sleeved shirt and worn out jeans, dabbing the sweat off his face, who looked alternately at the man hanging from the ceiling fan and at the police, licking his parched lips every now and then. "The boy called up the landlord. His son and a few others in the neighbourhood had to break the door open to get into the apartment. The boy has been here since the time the body was discovered."

Resting his back against the wall with one leg stretched forward and the other bent at the knees with the sole on the wall, Agni called the boy with a gesture. The boy approached him cautiously.

"What did you see here this morning?'"

Agni's question got him talking.

"Sir, I usually come here before eight in the morning. Sir used to open the door and collect the packets of milk," he gestured towards the lifeless body of Abhinav Mehra. "Today when I came here, I rang the bell, knocked on the door several times and called out for sir, but there was no response. I became worried and ran down to the ground floor. I spoke to Agarwal ji and his son came up here with me. He knocked a few times. He then went out, returned after a while with some more people from the neighbourhood and they broke in."

Agni turned to the doctor and the men from the forensics. The photographers were almost done.

"Doc, what would you say was the probable time of death?"

"I would say sometime between nine and twelve last night, Agni."

Agni turned his attention to Agarwal ji.

"When was the last time you saw Mr Mehra?"

"Well...he spent most of his time inside the apartment ever since the death of his wife. He was depressed. There was something bothering him...it was easy to figure out. I didn't see a lot of him over the last couple of weeks."

"Did he have visitors over the last couple of days?"

"I can't be too sure, I'm afraid," Agarwal ji looked almost apologetic for his lack of information about the final days of Abhinav Mehra.

"I understand," Agni reassured him.

He then asked him, "I'm assuming your tenants use the iron gate on the side?"

"Yes, yes. They have duplicate keys. I lock the gate after eleven in the night every day as also the door to the staircase leading to the first and second floor flats. I open them again in the morning when I wake up around six."

Arya smiled at Agni, "I think I know what you are thinking. A suicide doesn't turn you on enough, does it? Especially when that means you hit the dead end with one of the suspects of your investigation."

Agni replied, "Frankly Arya, Abhinav Mehra didn't look like someone who would kill himself with his wife's dupatta. He came across as someone far too composed for that. Yes... he did blame his work habits for the outcome of his marriage. But it looked like he was ready to move on. He talked about his work. He said there were business trips lined up."

"Agni, guilt often takes its own time to sink in. And when it does, it drives one to do the unimaginable."

"What guilt are we talking about here, Arya? That he did not spend quality time with his wife driving her to adultery, a life on the edge, and eventual murder? Or, are you suggesting—" Agni paused for a moment and looked at Arya, his eyes narrowed, "Are you suggesting, my friend, that we have here the murderer of Sheetal Mehra hanging from the ceiling?"

Arya smiled. "I won't be too surprised if that's what it turns out to be, if I have some understanding of the remorseful human mind."

On his way back to the police station, Agni noticed there had been a missed call from Priyanshi some time back. Agni remembered he had asked her the day before to find out who from Crescent Meenakshi Menon had met in the weeks before her death. Links, the all-important links the Professor had been talking about.

He called her back.

"I'm sorry I couldn't call you yesterday. I—" Priyanshi was going to offer an explanation. Agni had no patience for one.

"Who was it?" Agni jumped straight to the point.

"The meeting invites were sent out to a person by the name of Vikrant Mittal from Crescent. I tried to remember how he looked, but I am sorry I cannot help you with that. Ma'am met so many people in her office. But if I see him, I'll probably recognize him."

"Priyanshi, I need to find out more about Crescent's involvement in the bid that Meenakshi Menon was managing in her last days in office. Who in your office can tell me more about Crescent's role in that project? You mentioned a Senior Manager from Altius in the team."

Priyanshi said, "You can meet Raj...his full name is Raj Lohia. He is usually present in all discussions with vendors. In fact, I spoke to him yesterday after you had called and *he* mentioned Vikrant Mittal's name."

"Are you saying he was present in all meetings with Crescent?"

"Ma'am would always invite him to important meetings. It's very likely that he knows everything about Crescent's involvement in the project. By the way, when I spoke to him yesterday, he mentioned that he might have to go out of town for at least a week on a business tour. He had a flight to catch this morning."

"Thanks Priyanshi. You have no idea how much this helps. I will speak to him when he is back in Kolkata."

"Can I ask you something?"

"Go ahead!"

"Why did you want to know specifically about this company? Did they have anything to do with—"

Agni stopped her before she could finish. "We don't know for sure. But we will find out real soon. You have a great day, Priyanshi. And...and take very good care of yourself."

"Thank you, sir."

"You can call me Agni."

Day 17
10:00 a.m.

A rya walked into Agni's office to find him at his desk. He had a condescending smile on his face and a file in his hand.

Arya contemplated him for a while and then said restlessly, 'OK now...what is it?'

"The triumph of evidence over your slightly erroneous reading of the *remorseful human mind!*"

Agni stood up from his seat and pushed the file towards Arya along the desk. It was the autopsy report of Abhinav Mehra.

The removal of the dupatta had revealed a ligature mark on his neck right below the lower jaw. The mark was a couple of inches wide and circled the neck, forming a 'V' at the front and another at the back, suggesting that he had indeed been hanged. However, there was no haemorrhage surrounding the ligature mark suggesting that the injury from the ligature was inflicted *after* he had died.

On removing the high neck T-shirt, a second ligature mark was discovered around the victim's neck. The mark was an inch wide, dark red, and circled the neck, right below the Adam's apple. The skin above and below the mark showed signs of haemorrhage and had clearly been inflicted by a different ligature.

The cause of death was attributed to asphyxiation due to ligature strangulation, inflicted by the second ligature. The first ligature was, beyond doubt, post-mortem. The case was clearly one of homicide.

"What a bastard!" Arya thumped on the desk, referring to their unidentified adversary.

Agni stood in front of the desk – a picture of composure.

Agni went back to his chair and reflected aloud. "I believe the murderer was someone known to Abhinav Mehra. Allow me to reconstruct the likely sequence of events that night. Abhinav Mehra had unsuspectingly admitted the murderer in his apartment sometime in the evening. The murderer had obviously walked in through the open main gate. The murderer then strangled Abhinav at an opportune moment, made his death look like a suicide, locked the apartment door from outside and walked out well before eleven in the night, when Agarwal ji usually closes the main entrance.

"And he used the wife's dupatta to stage the suicide act, to make it look like an act of repentance."

Arya added, "And this was a well-planned act. No suspicious fingerprints anywhere. The murderer had himself covered."

Agni walked back to his desk and dialled Professor Parikshit Roy's number. He gestured at Arya to come closer. He turned the telephone speaker on.

"Good afternoon, Professor. Got a few minutes?"

"Agni!" the Professor exclaimed. "What a pleasure! You nabbed the killer?" the Professor sounded rather enthusiastic.

"On the contrary, Professor, there has been another murder."

"And what does that do to our *pattern*? I know I do keep coming back to that...but you see, that *is* important."

"It's a bit of an aberration, I'd say."

"In what ways?"

"The victim was Abhinav Mehra, the husband of Sheetal Mehra I talked to you about."

"And how did he die?"

"He was found hanging in his living room from a ceiling fan, his wife's *dupatta* around his neck."

The other end of the line went quiet for a few seconds. "Penance?" the Professor finally asked.

Arya cast a quick glance at Agni – *Look! It wasn't so stupid of me after all.*

"Well Professor, that's exactly what he had wanted us to believe. Arya is here with me and he was quite sure it was a suicide, in fact. But the autopsy report is in front of us. The report confirms that Abhinav Mehra was murdered and his death was made to look like a suicide prompted possibly by remorse."

"Hey Arya! Didn't realize you are around. You know, Arya, as we traverse the convoluted lanes and by-lanes of the human mind, we often tend to overlook the more obvious motives and implications of incidents around us. We often tend to be inclined towards a more romantic interpretation of incidents." The Professor laughed. "Don't beat yourself up for this, Arya."

The Professor asked, "So what does this mean for us, Agni?"

Agni thought for a while and said, "This really confirms our theory, Professor. There is someone out there, who does realize that his serial murders follow a pattern. He is following our investigation. He knows that it would not be too long before we find the pattern, analyse it, discover the invisible threads and come knocking at his door. He wanted to disrupt that pattern. Abhinav Mehra was killed to make the Sheetal Mehra murder look like an isolated case and not another link in the chain. One that started and ended with a marital discord over the wife's adultery, and an avenging husband later killing himself out of remorse."

"Exactly!" Professor Roy remarked approvingly, as if the best student in the class had come up with the correct answer to a tricky question. "The husband died a pawn's death. I'm sure the killer knew that the autopsy report would eventually prove that Abhinav had been murdered and that his death had been made to look like a suicide. Don't think even for a moment, Agni, that your adversary is naïve enough not to have realized that. He thought he was setting up a momentary distraction for you. Some killers love that. Playing mind games. Throwing the investigation off the track. Even if for a short while. Makes the cat-and-mouse game more exciting. He must be up to something nasty already."

Agni had no idea about the calamity that awaited him the next day.

Day 18
08:00 p.m.

" *Reached home. Getting ready to feed your hunger.*" Her message ended with two winks.

I smiled as I read her message on my phone while I sprayed the cologne. I was ready for our dinner date in her house.

We had met through a dating site on the Internet a few months back. I had checked the date on which she had put up her profile in the 'Married and Looking' section. It was a year back.

Now how many times have we been told not to trust strangers we meet on the Internet? Apparently she did not care. Her hunger for sex had probably blurred out her reasons. And the more they gave in to the craving, the weaker they became. Weak and miserable, they had no business staying alive. In the death of every adulteress like her, I felt peaceful deep inside. Even if that peace lasted only for a few days, till I was brutally snapped out of my slumber and ended up in the grip of hatred all over again.

I could not wait to take her in my arms, to play with her body, and then to see her dead, her filthy truth revealed before the world in death, the carefully crafted veneer torn to shreds.

Because the sense of relief from the last execution was fast running out. The restlessness was back. All I needed now was another dead woman. My fingers twitched with the desire to squeeze out another wretched life.

Agni Mitra, of course, was behind me. He was catching up, one false suspect from the Sheetal Mehra case already down, investigations heating up on the Meenakshi Menon case, the reality of Abhinav Mehra's death probably discovered by now. The executions, from now on, would have to be planned. Planned to the last detail. I could not afford to leave anything to chance from now on.

I had therefore studied the house and her movements over the last few days. I had to know the place like the back of my hand if I were to make a plan that was water tight. The best way was to take a walk around the neighbourhood. That way, I could observe a lot more than I could have by driving down the road in front of her house. And waiting near someone's house in a car was out of the question as it was bound to draw attention.

So I had walked around her house over the last few days, the water on the street sometimes past my ankles, my face hidden behind the hood of my raincoat that had been pulled over my head and had looked perfectly normal in the Kolkata monsoon. And I had everything planned out.

Just as I had done for Abhinav. I had nothing against him, but Agni Mitra needed some distraction, something to question his own theory. Something to deviate the course of the investigation. What fun!

There was the sound of loud thunder. The stage was set. I picked up my car key.

Day 18
11:30 p.m.

It was a while since Medha had left and Agni's life had been slipping into a mundane routine. He woke up at six, worked out, made breakfast for himself – mostly bread, boiled eggs and black coffee – went to work, picked up dinner on his way home, had a few drinks, and went to bed.

There was, however, one almost compulsive behaviour Agni hated himself for. His eyes kept looking for Medha wherever he went. A five-foot-something woman with straight hair – he had no idea there were so many of them in the city! He would see one next to his car on a busy road, driving a car herself or in the back seat of a car probably with a male companion. Or, he would walk briskly to catch up with one walking a few steps ahead of him with someone on the pavement. Or he would find someone on the escalator in a mall. Every time he felt an inexplicable sense of relief on discovering the woman was not Medha, and then, he would look around once again. He had never found himself in a similar state of mind. He both wanted and did not want to run into her. More importantly, Agni could not find a logical explanation for this behaviour of his.

At times he wished he had a girlfriend, just so that he could flaunt one, if and when he ran into Medha. He imagined the scene, scripted in his mind an exchange that would follow, and then wiped out those images from his mind, laughing to himself.

There were days when he remembered her affairs and her decision to walk out of the marriage and he felt extreme rage. And then there were days when his eyes turned moist when he heard a romantic song they had listened together in happier times. Agni was beginning to come to terms with that inconsistency in his feelings for her, now that they would never be together again. There was nothing he could do about the unpredictability of his feelings for that woman. He had better learn to accept them.

Agni had loaded his car with CDs of flippant dance numbers to escape from such mood swings for good.

It was one of those CDs that played loud as Agni drove from The Big Ben in Kenilworth on Theatre Road, the street lights reflected on rain-washed roads, making strange patterns. Agni thought he had probably had a couple of drinks too many, but Agni drove better when he was close to the edge. The whisky desensitized him to matters that would otherwise trouble his mind, and all his attention would usually be focused on the road for a change. The windows were rolled down, the wind was in his hair, and surprisingly, Medha was on his mind. Agni hated moments like this when she refused to leave his thoughts. He had been resisting the urge to text her from the moment the whisky had kicked in.

Agni stole a quick glance at his watch. It was close to midnight. And he was nearing Southern Avenue. "There's no reason why I can't drop in and say hello," Agni thought to himself. "She's surely not in bed so early." A part of him hated it; another gave in to the urge.

Agni knew the address. It didn't take him long to find Medha's house. He parked the car on the road and stepped out.

The door was locked. There was a calling bell on the wall next to it. Agni pressed it. Once, twice, thrice – the last time long enough for his fingertip to turn white. No response. Agni wondered if she was in.

He walked around the house. The windows were closed but the lights were on, though Agni could not look inside through the frosted glass on the windows. He reached the back of the house. The kitchen window was open and Agni managed to look inside. The kitchen opened to the dining space. The kitchen light was on, so was the light in the dining area. Medha would not keep all the lights on if she was to step out. The kitchen and dining areas must have been used recently. She was probably still in the house.

Agni dialled her number. And he could hear the phone ring somewhere inside the house. She was definitely inside.

But Medha did not take the call. Agni tried once again. Her phone kept ringing inside the house.

Agni was beginning to get worried. He could feel the sweat on his temples, trickling down the side of his face.

Agni called out her name a couple of times, but there was no response.

He walked up to his car, unlocked it and pulled out his Walther revolver and pushed it down the small of his back. He walked back to the front of the house.

It was an old fashioned house and as he pushed the wooden door across the middle, Agni realized it was just the lock in the centre that held the door shut. He moved a few steps back and landed his shoulder on the door, transferring his weight there. The door gave in a little. Two more shoves and the lock creaked.

A man patrolling the street saw him working on the door and ran up to him, wielding a stick, blowing on a whistle. Agni flashed his ID on his face, and shouted at him, "Stop the freaking music and give me a shoulder here." The two men hurled themselves on the door.

A dog on the road ahead had started protesting against the intrusion. Agni bent and picked up a stone and hurled it at the dog, making it run for cover. Two more heaves with their shoulders and the lock gave in with a clang.

His shirt drenched in sweat, Agni walked inside. The acid surged up his throat. He could feel the sweat trickling down his spine.

A narrow corridor opened up to a lighted living space. Sofa set around a low coffee table. The dining table further down. Agni could see plates and wine glasses. There was a bedroom to his right, curtain drawn aside, lights on.

Agni called out Medha's name and looked into the bedroom.

His heart froze. The moisture seemed to have evaporated from his mouth and his tongue felt heavy. He could hear the watchman's stick drop to the ground behind him. It seemed to Agni that the sound came from some place very far away.

The bed sheet was crumpled, pillows were scattered all around. Medha lay close to the edge of the bed. One of her legs was on the bed, folded at the knee. The other hung past the edge and fell short of the ground. She was in a nightwear that was raised well past her knees. One of the straps was off her shoulder, almost down to her elbow, revealing a bare breast. Her hair was open. The eyes almost popped out of her pale face, the mouth gaping – obvious signs of suffocation.

Agni checked for the non-existent pulse. Her lifeless black pupils were fixed in his direction. He stepped a few inches back.

Agni did not have to be told that Medha was dead.

Day 19
01:00 a.m.

A gni asked the watchman not to touch anything and walked down to the living area. He fished out his mobile phone and made a call to Inspector Siddharth Rajan. The area was under his jurisdiction.

"Hey Agni, what's up?"

"Sid, where are you?"

"I'm home. Why?"

"You need to come down to this address." Agni rattled off the address and added, "As soon as you can make it."

"What's the matter, Agni? Whose house is that?"

"Sid," Agni took his time, "It's Medha's house. I'm in her flat right now."

"What about her? Is everything alright?"

"She's dead, Sid."

The other side of the line went quiet as Inspector Siddharth searched for words.

"I-I'm sorry, Agni," he finally mumbled.

"Sid, come down as soon as you can. I'm waiting." Agni ended the call.

Agni wondered for a minute if this was all a bad dream, and if he would hear his alarm clock in a minute and wake up with a start on his own bed, in his own room. But none of that happened.

Agni's legs felt heavy as he tried to get up from the chair. As if in a trance, he pulled himself across the room to the dining table. Plates and wine glasses. For two. Medha had had a visitor who must have gagged her to death.

It was then that his eyes were drawn to a scribbling in red on the wall adjacent to the table. The letters ended in streams of red fluid down the wall. Agni moved closer.

Agni – Don't Take This Personally

Agni could feel his eyes burning. His temples throbbed as the blood surged to his brain. The sweat formed rivulets on his face. He thrust his head back and screamed till his throat burnt as if someone had poured molten lead down it. As his anger spread like venom through his veins, his muscles tensed. With the drool dripping past the corners of his mouth, he landed two pile-driving punches on the wall ahead.

Day 19
02:00 a.m.

It was raining when Inspector Siddharth Rajan reached Medha's house in Southern Avenue. In no time, the bedroom was teeming with policemen, photographers, a doctor and people from the forensics laboratory.

Agni stood at the door and looked inside. He looked at the men in the room and looked back at Medha. He wished he could walk up to her and cover her up with one of the sheets that were folded neatly in a cupboard close to the bed. But that was not to be. Like the rest of his victims, the killer had managed to reduce Medha to an obscene spectacle before the world.

The doctor walked up to Agni and said, "I'm sorry, sir. I am told she was once married to you."

"She was...till about a month back," Agni whispered, his voice almost inaudibly broken. "What does it look like, Doctor?"

"I will put the time between nine and eleven in the night. She was choked to death, possibly by one of the pillows there."

"Thanks, Doctor. I will get in touch with you later if I have more questions."

"Of course, sir. Please accept my condolences."

Agni nodded, still staring at the body on the bed. The doctor walked away.

Agni was left to himself once again. He was finding it difficult to come to terms with the fact that Medha was lying dead before his eyes. He had never in his life imagined that he would have to deal with Medha's death as a very public event, as yet another link in a chain of serial murders.

The circumstances of her death were a crude reminder to her lifestyle. Leaning against the door frame with his eyes fixed on the scantily-dressed body on the bed, one moment Agni blamed himself, the next moment he fumed in anger at her decision to leave him and live her life on the edge. But above all those inconsistent emotions, his hatred for the killer was the only constant – unbridled and overpowering.

Agni had asked one of the men from the laboratory to check the writing on the wall. He came back.

"It's the wine, sir. And no fingerprints. Probably had gloves on."

Agni clenched his fist and thumped on the other palm. The man retracted.

When Siddharth came up to him, Agni said, "Sid, I need to be alone for some time. I'll leave now. I'll call you later."

Before crossing the main door, he stopped in his tracks and turned round. He called out to Siddharth and said, "You may want to look into her laptop and mobile phone. Those could help. She had many friends, and I won't vouch for any of those scoundrels."

Agni did realize that Medha's laptop and mobile phone records would perhaps reveal nasty secrets of her private life, but at that moment, there was nothing in the world that mattered to him more than getting his hands on any clue that could lead him to the killer.

Agni had to raise his hands to guard his eyes from the glare of flash bulbs even as the microphones were thrust towards him. He could not see them, he could not hear what any one of them asked. He could not care less – the hatred was mutual. The only difference was that Agni could afford to ignore them, but they could not afford to ignore Agni.

He walked right into the middle of the crowd of TV and press reporters and grabbed the first microphone he could reach.

Raising his broken voice several notches, Agni looked unseeingly at the hordes of faces before him and screamed, "I'm coming for you, you bastard. You've brought the battle to my backyard."

Cameras flashed, more questions followed from frenzied reporters. Agni did not pay heed. When a reporter from one of the TV channels chased him almost to his car, Agni turned towards her and shouted into her face, "Wasn't that enough for breaking news?" he paused and whispered menacingly on her face. "Now go peddle her death for your freaking TRPs. Oh, and look at you...do you *ever* forget the make-up?"

Leaving her speechless, Agni jumped into his car and drove away with a screech.

Day 19
03:30 a.m.

As he sat in the balcony of his apartment looking at the rain-soaked darkness, Agni remembered what Medha had asked him the last time they had met in his apartment. On hearing that Agni had gone drinking after witnessing the horrible death of Sheetal Mehra, she had asked him, "Isn't it surprising that it's the only way you can handle your emotions?" And her voice had climbed a notch.

Agni had never in his life imagined a situation like the one he had at the moment, and he had never been too sure if he would indeed be sorry for Medha when she died. But the subconscious has its own ways of responding to situations and events. Agni instinctively picked up the bottle of whisky and took a long swig.

He thought he could hear the clicks of Medha's high heels reverberating in the corridor. Those sounds had marked her exit from his life as she had walked down the corridor the last time they had met right there in his apartment. Agni ran his fingers through his wet dishevelled hair. "Stupid bitch!" he muttered under his breath

Agni had not realized when he had fallen asleep. When he woke up, he was still in the balcony of his apartment. The rains had stopped sometime during the night, but it was quite cold. He had a dull headache. Everything around him seemed damp and melancholy.

He looked at the watch. It was almost five. He walked to the toilet, relieved himself, gingerly made his way to the bedroom and fell on the bed on his back. But sleep evaded him.

That was the bed where Medha and Agni had spent nights shouting at each other and fighting like alley cats, often over issues that seemed so trivial when Agni looked back now. And that was the bed where they had made love night after night. Towards the end of their marriage, their lovemaking had been reduced to a domestic routine that they would indulge in a few times every month, just because a healthy married couple was supposed to, and to satisfy a physical need just as someone sits on the pot every morning to empty one's bowels or munches on a sandwich in the afternoon to satiate one's hunger. But there had been times when making love to Medha was a passionate experience, where they could sense the union of their souls and not just of two bodies, and they would often end up teary-eyed. He missed that – he missed that sorely.

Agni tried to calculate how many times they had made love. There was no way to figure out. Did *she* keep track? She would often surprise Agni by effortlessly quoting from memory the number of days that had passed since the last time they had made love. The intervals would most often be several weeks mostly because Agni had been too tired after his work or had been away from home investigating a murder. Which meant she did keep track. How *did* she? Did she write down the dates somewhere? Did she make tally marks? Agni wished he knew. It was too late now.

Agni slipped into a slumber again.

When he woke up again, Agni picked up his phone and looked at the time. It was close to seven in the morning. The light seeping in through cracks in the window curtain above the bed was feeble. The new day looked despondent. Or, maybe it was just him. He looked at the sky. It was a dull grey. He stayed awake, staring at the ceiling for some time. And then, he reached for the phone. Agni did not know why, but he scrolled down to Priyanshi's number and typed, "He killed my ex-wife last night."

Day 19
09:00 a.m.

"I'm sorry to hear about Medha, Agni. I know the two of you were not—"

Agni did not let Professor Parikshit Roy finish. "Professor, I am sorry for the really short notice. But I had to see you this morning."

Agni had called the Professor in the morning and had asked for his time. He had picked up Arya on the way. And the two of them had reached Professor Parikshit Roy's house as quickly as the Kolkata traffic on a busy morning had allowed. The Professor, of course, had to leave for his clinic but Agni had promised that he would not take more than half an hour. Agni was therefore in a hurry to cut to the chase. His anger was the emotion uppermost in his mind and he could not care less for condolences.

His eyes were red, anger simmering in them. His hair was dishevelled, the stubble was a day old, and the sweat-stained shirt from last night was untucked over his jeans with its sleeves rolled up. Agni looked unkempt, but intimidating. Professor Roy understood what Agni was going through and chose to let him speak his mind, without caring for niceties.

"Professor, why the hell do you think he is doing this?" Agni clenched his teeth as he spoke.

Professor Roy reclined on his seat, took a long drag of the cigar, thought for a while and said, "You know, Agni, this pattern is not unfamiliar to me. If you look closely, there is a common message that the murderer seems to be delivering through his acts. Simply put, the underlying message seems to be – and please don't mind my saying this under the present circumstances – the woman is an adulteress and she is left to die, shamelessly exposed to the world."

"No question of taking it personally, Professor. We all know the kind of life Medha lived," Agni looked at Arya, who lowered his head. "We know for sure that at least three of them, including Medha, were adulteresses," Agni confirmed.

"There are multiple instances of such behaviour in all these tomes of criminal psychology," Professor Roy pointed at the towering bookcases that covered the walls at the far end of his sitting room. "And such behaviours are caused by a variety of reasons. The person may have been a victim of betrayal, rejection or some form of adultery himself, possibly because of a woman. And now he is out to exact his revenge. The roots of such evils are most often to be traced in the childhood or early years of a person's life."

"So are you saying, Professor, that this man is *seeking out* adulteresses and killing them?"

"That could be the case for some of these murders, where his actions look pre-mediated. For the others, it may also be that he does not really approach these women with the intention of killing them. Maybe he simply meets women, succumbs to temptations, as any normal person like you and I may, under specific circumstances. And, in the process, he is *reminded of similar situations from his past*, which may have left deep scars in his psyche, and ends up killing these women, almost as a retaliation against those women he remembers."

"So, what you are saying is that some of these murders could be impulsive, some could be pre-mediated, even though the motive behind each of them is eventually the same."

"Yes, that would most likely be the case. And are you making progress in discovering the links among these murders?"

Arya spoke, "Professor, we now have information that Vikrant Mittal was involved in discussions with Meenakshi Menon regarding an upcoming project in Altius Finance. They had met a couple of times before her murder. That, for sure, is a link."

"Excellent! I would say you should step up your vigil on Mittal. And do keep me informed." Professor Roy stole a glance at his watch.

Agni read the signal. He stood up, shook the Professor's hand and walked out restlessly with Arya in tow.

Day 19
02:00 p.m.

"So what did you find in Medha's house?" Agni asked Inspector Siddharth as he later walked into his office and sat across the table.

"Agni, Medha obviously had a visitor that night," Siddharth paused.

Agni sensed his hesitation and said, "Sid, as I mentioned to you earlier, there is nothing personal about this. Let's keep this strictly professional and talk just as we would about any other investigation. I saw the plates and the wine glasses myself."

Siddharth was somewhat reassured and continued more confidently, "There was no sign of any forced entry into the house. There were plates and wine glasses on the table, as you mentioned, suggesting that they had dinner together in the house. So the person in question is obviously someone she knew. The killer had wiped his fingerprints off the glasses. Most of the prints around the house are Medha's. This was definitely a pre-mediated murder, Agni. The killer came prepared.

"You had a view of the bedroom. As the doctor mentioned to you, she was suffocated to death possibly by one of the pillows that you saw scattered on that bed.

"When the killer left, he pulled the main door from the outside, locking it in the process." Siddharth paused.

"Did you go through her laptop? What about call records from her mobile phone?"

"We are getting her call records checked. As for the laptop, I did a preliminary scan and there was nothing out of the ordinary that caught my attention. I wanted to ask you, Agni, what exactly do you have in mind? Are we looking for something specific?"

Agni took time to respond. "I know she spent a lot of time on the Internet when she was home. If we don't find anything important in that laptop, I would suggest we get the cyber cell involved. I have a feeling her e-mail account and her social media activities would yield valuable clues."

Siddharth was quiet for some time, looking away from Agni. Then he turned to Agni and said, "Are you sure about this? There is nothing personal going on here, I hope?"

Agni looked at Siddharth in the eyes and thumped on his desk. "Sid, you know me for years, goddammit! I'd never involve the cyber cell to snoop into my dead ex-wife's e-mails. So far as Medha and I are concerned, we were finished long before she got killed. We were legally divorced, for God's sake!" Agni paused for a minute and pulled himself together, taking a sip of the black coffee in front of him.

He went on, "Sid, I am going to tell you this not with the intention of maligning my ex-wife who is now dead, but to help our investigation. I always knew she was going around sleeping with men and I never asked for their names. It didn't matter to me who those men were. But, as you can see, it was someone she had invited to her house to spend the night with, who had a good meal, probably had a romp in the bed with her and then gagged her to death. And chances are that her call records, especially for that day and that night, and records of her online interactions with her friends would possibly yield vital clues to who that man is. Still have doubts about my intentions here, Sid?"

Siddharth placed a hand on Agni's shoulder. "Calm down, Agni. I'm sorry if my comment ended up offending you but that was never my intention. I do see your point and I will get the cyber cell involved right away. I will get in touch with you when I hear back from them.

"But you know that the cyber cell may take a while. They are reeling under backlogs and then there are bureaucratic processes to deal with. Also if the murderer communicated with her online from behind proxy servers, or from neighbourhood cyber cafés where most of the time identity proofs are not checked, it would be very difficult to get to him."

"Yes, Sid. I am completely aware of the challenges. I'm not suggesting that we should rely solely on the records of her online activities and her call records to get to the killer. But that should not stop us from making an effort. And hey, sorry about that reaction. It's just not easy—"

Siddharth interrupted Agni, "You don't need to explain, Agni. I understand. I know about the other cases you have on your plate right now. And then, having to cope with this."

"Well, these are not separate cases any more, Sid. We have just one case on our hands now and these are crumbs of the same goddamned pie. And we will all work together to get to the guy. I would also suggest we engage the lab to carry out exhaustive DNA tests on Medha's body – a swab for DNA samples on her body, DNA profiling of hair samples, and DNA profiling of any skin cells that might have been detected under her nails. I have initiated a similar process for the Sheetal Mehra case. Again, I am aware of the time involved and the various constraints, but those should not deter us from taking a more scientific approach in our investigation. There is a high probability that the DNA reports will point to the same person. That will work in our favour whenever the trial comes up."

Siddharth nodded and excused himself. After he left, Agni called Arya to his office. He updated Arya with details of the investigation into Medha's murder, mentioning specifically his instructions to Inspector Siddharth to look into Medha's mobile phone records and online activities. He asked Arya to gather more information about the murder of the housewife in Salt Lake that he had reported earlier. There had to be a connection of that incident with the rest of the cases.

Agni then made a call to Inspector Vishwajeet. He shared with him his findings in the Meenakshi Menon murder case, highlighting the Crescent connection, and putting that case in the context of the murder reported in Salt Lake, the murder of Sheetal Mehra and that of her husband, and the previous day's murder of his ex-wife. They agreed that they should gather more information about the nature of involvement of Crescent and more specifically, Vikrant Mittal, in the tender that Meenakshi Menon had been managing prior to her murder.

The next call was to Priyanshi. When she picked up the phone, Agni said, "I'm sorry I probably woke you up with my message this morning. I have no idea why I did that!"

"It's alright Agni. I'm sorry to hear about her. Are you alright?"

"Thanks, Priyanshi. Yes, I'm fine. Well...I've been on my own for a while now. Ever since she left me."

"I can understand." Priyanshi paused for a while and said, "Are you back to work? You sound...well, how do I say this... very business-like."

"I won't rest until I find him."

Day 19
09:00 p.m.

Vikrant returned to the living room from the toilet with a towel, wiping the sweat off his bare torso, with a grin of satisfaction on his face.

"Couldn't take my eyes off you in the office today. I could hardly wait."

Vaishali stood up from the couch and lowered her skirt. He fondled her over her skirt as she crossed his way, walking nonchalantly towards the refrigerator, pushing aside with her foot the panty she had discarded on the floor sometime back.

"Get the beer now," Vikrant barked his order.

"Have the cops spoken to you recently?" Vaishali asked as she handed him a bottle.

"Why do you care?" Vikrant questioned back.

"I was wondering—"

Vikrant did not let her finish, "By the way, I've been thinking of asking you this for a while...the cops also know about the committee. Was it you who told them about it?" Vikrant sounded concerned.

"No way, Vikrant! How could you even imagine I would tell them about it?" Vaishali looked shocked, "I talked about her bad marriage and all the men she had been seeing. And I also mentioned that her husband had been at the party that evening."

"That throws up a whole bunch of suspects. That was smart of you! Well...the husband of course is out of reach now," Vikrant laughed. He became serious again and asked, "Who do you think mentioned the committee to the cops then?"

"One of the cops had been in the office asking questions."

Vikrant spoke to himself, "In any case, that committee could prove nothing. What a bitch! She goes around sleeping with anything that moves, and then goes and puts in a complaint against *me*!" Vikrant made no attempt to hide his contempt for his departed colleague.

Vikrant put an arm around Vaishali.

"She had no idea what Vikrant Mittal could have done for her if only she had cared to keep him happy," Vikrant winked. "Well, I don't expect everyone to be as smart as you are," he pulled Vaishali closer.

"Vikrant, you know I want to get away from all this. You said you would propose my name for the project in France."

Vikrant looked irritated. "How many times do I have to tell you? Do *not* ask for these favours right after you have had sex with me. You make yourself sound like a whore asking to be paid. There is a time and place for everything. Plus, until and unless the investigations are over, you aren't going anywhere out of Kolkata in any case."

Vikrant put the empty beer bottle down and pulled Vaishali closer. As he started rubbing his nose along the sides of her neck, Vaishali's tired eyes were fixed on a framed picture next to the couch.

Later that evening, as Vikrant walked out of Vaishali's apartment and got into his BMW 3 Series, he did not notice a Swift several feet behind. The Swift was parked on the road in front of Vaishali's apartment all the time Vikrant was with her. The car started almost at the same time as Vikrant did, and then followed him maintaining a safe distance from his car. As he started driving, the man in the Swift dialled a number. The call was received at the other end by Inspector Arya Sen.

Day 21
09:30 a.m.

*A*s I drove towards the office, my eyes relishing the views of empty New Town roads stretching to the horizon, variously coloured high-rises against the backdrop of open skies and the hues of green all around me, I felt at peace.

I remembered the grotesque face of Medha sprawled on her bed, and I felt at peace. The helpless wail of Agni Mitra speaking to the TV cameras rang in my ears and I felt triumphant. How often does one get to see 'The Agni Mitra' make an ass of himself in front of the cameras like he did that night? That was my moment of glory.

It was during dinner that she mentioned that she had been married to Agni Mitra, who was an Assistant Commissioner with Kolkata Police – 'the' Agni Mitra. I almost choked on the pasta – had to reach for a sip of the wine. The woman in skimpy nightwear digging into her pasta right in front of me suddenly looked every bit a prize catch! That she would not live to see the next day was a given. That Agni Mitra, hot on the trail of his 'ruthless adversary' (is that how he would love to address me?) would turn up at the 'venue' was a given, as well. What gave me the extra kick was the realization that here was my chance to 'get personal' with him. The writing on the wall was an improvisation but had a touch of class about it.

I was surely getting better at this. I had elevated the executions almost to the level of fine art. You see, every time I killed someone, I made mental notes. Of what worked, what did not work. And learnt from my experiences. It was also important to slow down at times. Take a step back, relish the success, marvel at my own finesse.

I remembered the first one.

Well, that one was different from the rest in many ways. The prey, of course, was easy. I can still sense with all my heart and soul the pure satisfaction of seeing her drop to her death through the steel cold night air. And the cover of the night helped.

But there were so many things not quite right about it.

I thought it was over too soon, like clumsy first time sex between teenagers in high school. And then I was scared. I had not even planned for that one, for God's sake! It was all in that one moment. That rush! That impulse! What if I had messed up? What if she had only been injured? What if she came back to tell?

And then the remorse. For days, I kept talking to myself. Justifying. Reasoning. Reminding myself of all the wrongs that I had silently endured for months with her and for years before that, with all the other women destiny had mercilessly thrown my way. Reassuring myself that justice had finally been delivered. And justice was no different from revenge. And I slowly came around. I congratulated myself on my first success.

And then I remembered the first time I had seen her.

The year was 2013. My heart skipped several beats when I saw her for the first time in a Durga Puja pandal in Kolkata, *wearing a pink sari with the charming discomfort of a girl not quite used to wearing one, her hair cascading down her back. She had come down to our neighbourhood to catch up with old friends, she told me later. Our eyes had met several times before we were introduced to each other by common friends.*

As they say, one does not find one's soulmate. A soulmate 'happens' unannounced in some turn of the deliciously unpredictable journey called 'life', when one is not even ready for the occasion. Love caught us unawares as our eyes talked and our hearts made silent promises, with loudspeakers blaring, and sounds of frenzied beating of the drums filling the evening air.

The next few months turned out to be the best of my life. There was a reason to leave office early and the weekends were worth waiting for.

We would talk for hours and when we met in our favourite coffee shop after work, the table in one corner of the shop would be ours till they pulled the shutters down. We went shopping together, we explored all the restaurants in town, and we did not miss a single movie.

The impatience with which I waited to see her every day, the jealousy I felt when other men looked at her, the eagerness with which I reached for my phone to text her and let her know I had been thinking of her every time it rained and the earth smelt sweet, and then the restlessness I felt while waiting for her replies to my texts – were emotions I had never felt before and had never imagined, in the wildest of my dreams, that I ever would.

We kissed for the first time in a movie hall. It was spontaneous and my heart throbbed wildly all the while. We kissed through the entire length of a romantic song we had been humming together over the last few days while walking back home late in the evenings through the fog, along the lonely lanes and by-lanes of the city, fingers locked, our palms sweating together.

As we kissed, I opened my eyes for a fleeting second and saw her – eyes closed, a few strands of hair on her face, light and shadows playing on the face alternately as the scenes changed on the screen, and I had never seen anything more beautiful. And then my eyes closed again.

I realized for the first time that a kiss could make one giddy. It could make one lose sense of time and place. The kiss that evening also made me realize how much I loved her and I wanted her to be mine for life. Mine and no one else's.

We moved in together against the wishes of our families early last year. Not that we cared. We told the landlord that we were married. He never doubted us.

We set up our little nest with child-like fervour. We looked forward to going back home after work. The restaurants in the city missed us sorely as I loved everything she cooked. It was the first time she cooked for anyone and she loved the way I tried to help her in the kitchen with my pathetic culinary skills. We would spend evenings in each other's arms listening to our favourite songs or just talking about our childhood. We would make slow passionate love and then fall asleep in each other's arms every night. We would wake up warm, huddled in each other's arms, and then, rush through our morning chores, getting ready for work, landing up in the shower together. And we would be in touch with each other all day on our phones and Facebook, exchanging sweet nothings – sometimes mushy, sometimes naughty – waiting for the day to end so we could rush back to our nest. With her, even grocery shopping was fun.

Life had never looked more beautiful. We had never looked more beautiful. And my dark memories were beginning to fade.

While there were those odd nights few and far between when my stepmother and Anita haunted my dreams, all that was left of my memories of the schoolgirl I had a crush on, was the image of her speeding away down that dusty narrow lane on a bike hugging a different boy every few months. Every time a nightmare woke me up, I crawled to the warmth of the bosom of the woman sleeping next to me and went back to sleep in peace.

And then everything changed.

Day 21
10:30 a.m.

It was ten in the morning when Raj Lohia walked into Agni's office. Agni figured out Raj was in his forties, of medium height, had a bald pate, a French-cut beard that made his round face look slightly longer, and he wore glasses with a thick black frame. He was in a crisp blue shirt and black trousers.

Arya and Vishwajeet were also in the room.

Raj greeted them with firm shakes of his hand.

Agni started the conversation. "Mr Lohia, we are investigating the murder of Ms Meenakshi Menon, who used to be the Director of Information Systems in Altius Finance. I wanted to ask you a few questions. I understand you are a Senior Manager with the company."

"That's correct, Officer. And I heard about the investigation from Priyanshi. You had asked for the names of people from the IT companies Ma'am had met in the weeks before her death."

"I had, indeed. And she wanted me to talk to you for more information about those meetings." Agni paused briefly and then asked, "So what exactly do you do at Altius Finance, Mr Lohia?"

"I manage the development and installation of software within the firm. I also worked with Ma'am evaluating the different software and hardware vendors and system integrators. The evaluation is mandatory before we take purchasing decisions."

"How long have you been with this firm?"

"Close to three years."

"In your capacity as a Senior Manager in the organization directly responsible for the hardware and software purchases, may I assume that your involvement is mandatory in any bid process?"

"That's right."

"And how do you actually evaluate these vendors?" Agni was bent over the table, his fingertips arched on his chin. He appraised Raj Lohia with narrow eyes.

"Well...in many cases, before awarding the entire deal to a particular vendor and asking it to develop a system for the entire organization, we ask the vendor to develop a pilot solution for a particular division. It's my responsibility to oversee such pilot projects, evaluate them and report back to the management on whether the particular vendor is an appropriate choice for the larger implementation."

"Which means decisions worth crores of rupees rest on your shoulders." Agni smiled.

"You can say that." Raj's face lighted up with the realization that he had managed to impress upon the three policemen the importance of his position in the firm.

"And would you have the final say all the time?"

Raj kept quiet for a few seconds. "Not always, you know. There are several other considerations, not necessarily technical, that go into certain procurement decisions. I wouldn't know about them."

"And who would, in such cases?" Agni probed further.

"Well, Ma'am took a lot of those decisions in consultation with the Purchase Division or other stakeholders, where the criteria were not purely technical. You know, we have budget allocated at the start of the financial year. We need to complete our programs within the budget."

"I can imagine." Agni reclined in his chair, wrinkles on his forehead. What Raj Lohia had just said implied that there were probably those odd instances where Meenakshi Menon exercised her authority to take purchasing decisions herself, citing commercial or strategy reasons, ignoring recommendations from the technical team. Agni tried to relate that observation with what he had heard from Priyanshi. One could not rule out the possibility that there might have been instances when her reasons had not been entirely official.

"So what are you working on these days, Mr Lohia?" Agni asked.

"Well," Raj Lohia hesitated for a moment, "If you are looking for detailed information, then you'd have to excuse me. There are confidentiality issues that—"

Agni sensed his predicament and said, "I'm not really looking for any classified information, Mr Lohia. My intention is not to cause any ethical dilemma for you. Let me be more specific. I would like to know if in her last days, Ms Meenakshi Menon was working on a new project and whether a tender was issued for the same."

Raj Lohia looked reassured. "Yes, she was. We, as a matter of fact, have a target of overhauling our customer relationship management systems by end of this year and we issued a tender to identify a suitable IT service provider to do that work for us."

Agni came straight to the point, "And was Crescent Technologies one of the vendors in the race? I believe they operate from the same premises as yours in the New Town area."

Raj Lohia exclaimed, "Well yes! I am assuming you found that out from Ma'am's meeting records."

Agni smiled, "I did. And can I assume that you were present in all the meetings that Ms Meenakshi Menon had with Crescent?"

"I was. Ma'am had wanted me to."

"I understand. And I believe it was Mr Vikrant Mittal who represented Crescent in those discussions."

"Yes. He leads the Kolkata operations of Crescent and represented his company in the discussions."

"Do you remember how many meetings were conducted with Crescent?"

"We met Crescent thrice. The first one had been an introductory meeting where we had informed Mr Mittal that Crescent had been shortlisted along with two other companies for the work we had planned this year. The overhaul of the customer relationship management system, as you would understand, would have significant impact on the way we do our business. As such, the management had decided to try it out on a controlled scale. We wanted the shortlisted vendors to come up with ideas for a pilot implementation. The final decision on the vendors is still pending, by the way." Raj Lohia paused and took a sip from the glass of water that had been placed before him. He then continued, "In the second meeting, I had explained to them what the pilot implementation was expected to deliver, and in the third, they presented their ideas. In fact, the third meeting was a couple of days before Ma'am's death."

"So there were two meetings over the two weeks preceding the death of Ms Meenakshi. Do you confirm?"

"Yes. Those were the second and the third meetings with Crescent, as I told you just now."

"Was Mr Vikrant Mittal present in *all* these meetings?"

"He was present in all of them," Raj confirmed.

"And did you have further meetings with Mr Vikrant Mittal after Ms Meenakshi's death?"

"Not really. I have spoken to Mr Mittal a few times on the phone. But everything is in a bit of turmoil right now, as you can understand. Someone will step in for Ma'am. The final decision on the project will be on hold till then."

"I understand. It was all too sudden and unexpected." Agni stood up. "Well, Mr Lohia, thanks for all the information. You have been very helpful."

After Raj Lohia had walked out, Agni looked at Arya and Vishwajeet and said with a smirk, "It's not too difficult to imagine Meenakshi Menon falling for the charms of the debonair Vikrant Mittal, is it? And our man must have only been too happy to oblige!"

Day 21
3:00 p.m.

Vikrant Mittal was busy with his mobile phone when the phone on his desk rang. He cast a cursory glance at the display. It was Dhruv Bakshi, the HR Director.

Vikrant turned on the speaker and brought his face closer to the phone.

"Good afternoon, Dhruv," Vikrant tried hard not to let his curiosity reach his voice.

"I don't have good news for you Vikrant, I'm afraid." Dhruv did not bother to get into niceties.

"What is it this time?" Vikrant threw in a forced chuckle, trying to make light of the situation. Something in Dhruv's tone told him this was not going to be an easy conversation.

"Fresh reports of your sexual escapades with the ladies in the office, Vikrant."

Vikrant picked up the receiver, cutting off the speaker. He opened his mouth, trying to voice a meek protest but Dhruv did not let him speak and went on, "I'm sick and tired with this now! E-mails have been sent out to everyone who matters in the senior management by three ladies this morning, and there is damning evidence this time. I have been checking facts all this while myself. Obscene e-mails that you have written to them over months, voice recordings and there is a video as recent as last weekend. You were being filmed Vikrant! What on earth were you thinking?" Vikrant could hear Dhruv thumping his desk.

"Look Dhruv...this is all a sham. It's nothing but a bloody conspiracy! Just like last time!" Vikrant sounded helpless as he licked his parched lips. He loosened his tie, his shirt drenched to his skin in sweat.

"Just shut up, Vikrant! Don't try my patience! I have orders to set up a committee...*again!* Though I personally don't see the need for one. You deserve to be kicked out right now! But we need to play by the book." Dhruv paused for breath and then continued, "You are suspended with immediate effect, Vikrant. I will let you know when you need to report before the committee. Leave your office...*Now!* You are disgusting!" Vikrant heard the line go dead at the other end.

As he put the phone down, Vikrant Mittal felt a buzzing sound in his ears. The walls in his room seemed to be closing in on him. He felt breathless.

Day 21
08:00 p.m.

Agni was with Arya and Vishwajeet when Siddharth called him.

"Agni, I have news for you. The cyber cell is working on Medha's laptop and details of her online activities. They have initiated the process of securing access to her e-mail accounts and social networks on the Internet. However, from her browsing history, it seems she was a regular on several online dating sites. We are working on securing access to those accounts as well.

"In the meantime, we have also checked call records from her mobile phone over the last one month. The numbers of messages and calls to one particular number show a significant rise over the last few weeks, including several calls made and messages exchanged on the day and the night of the incident. The number belongs to a woman by the name of Niharika Basu."

Agni's eyebrows were wrinkled. "A woman?"

"Yes, a woman. The mobile company has passed her address on to us. It's a house in Moore Avenue in South Kolkata. There was no one at that address when I went there this afternoon. I am planning to drop in one more time tomorrow morning. Do you want to come along?"

"Of course. I will come down to your office."

Agni put the phone down and told Arya and Vishwajeet what he had just heard.

Arya looked surprised, "A woman? Are you sure we got the right number?"

Agni got up from his chair and paced up and down the room, his arms behind him.

"I don't see any reason to doubt that." He was silent for a couple of minutes and then he stopped in his tracks.

He turned to Arya and exclaimed, "Arya, do you remember we talked about the possibility of the killer having an accomplice, someone who's creating circumstances favourable for him to commit these crimes involving all these women, or helping him confuse us?"

Arya's face lit up. "Of course we did, Agni!" he exclaimed.

Agni's eyes shone, "And we have confirmed reports from your informer that at least one man in Crescent is having a clandestine affair with his female colleague. We have already seen that the lady, in turn, is also quite protective about his reputation."

Day 21
09:00 p.m.

Vaishali Arora took a shower and came out in the balcony of her third floor apartment. She sat down on the hammock and took a sip of the chilled beer, her iPod plugged into her ears. There was a light drizzle and the breeze was refreshing. The traffic on Ballygunje Circular Road was characteristically sparse.

Vikrant had been having his way with her for months with false promises of pulling the right strings and recommending her for the company's projects in France.

"The timing has to be right. It's all about timing you know," he would say.

Vaishali had been blinded by her ambitions. She had believed in Vikrant and in his false promises of an easy road to prosperity. She had played along. And she had been betrayed.

When she had reached office the day before, she had found Preeti waiting for her at her seat with a box of laddoos. Preeti was a couple of years her junior. Vaishali had been Preeti's mentor in her early days in the firm.

Vaishali had picked one up and asked, "What are the laddoos for, Preeti? Taking the plunge finally? Your mom must be over the moon!"

"On the contrary, she has stopped talking to me since last night. I'm all set to run away from her stupid proposals. At least for two years!" Preeti had dropped the box of laddoos on the desk in a hurry and had thrown up her arms triumphantly, her smile lighting up her face. "I'm off to France! At least for two years!"

Vaishali had asked her about the assignment. Same client. Same project. Same position that Vikrant had promised to her several months back. Vaishali had somehow managed to congratulate Preeti without her disappointment and her hurt showing on her face. She had then stormed into Vikrant's office demanding an explanation.

Vikrant had literally thrown his hands up and said, "It was a collective decision by the management. I did try to build a case for you, sweetheart, but there was general consensus about Preeti being the right person for the job. Plus, you are not in a position to leave the country till the investigations get over. The project cannot wait for you. Luckily for her, Preeti was not in the party that night, you see."

Vaishali had walked out of his cabin.

She had gone back home and cried. She had no idea for how long. She had screamed inside her lonely house, cursing herself for letting Vikrant Mittal trample her dignity for months in that very room, on that very couch.

There was a framed picture next to that couch. In that picture, Vaishali had her arms around Abhinav and Sheetal, both of them in their wedding attire. That picture was a reminder of the harsh reality of Vaishali's life – that she had lost Abhinav, the man she loved with all her heart and soul, to her friend Sheetal.

"It was so foolish of me to think that I was taking revenge on Abhinav, putting that goddamned picture there on the table and having sex with my lecherous boss right in front of his eyes. Even after he died!" Vaishali had lamented in the darkness of her room that evening, "And I've been an idiot thinking every time he had me right here on this couch, that I was getting closer to the good life. What I should have realized is that he must have been banging other girls in the office as well, and that we were all in a race where the result could swing anyone's way. Vikrant probably had nothing to do with the decision in the first place."

When she reached office that morning, she called the girls she knew were close to Vikrant, for a meeting in the cafeteria. Preeti was absent. Three of the girls owned up to having had sex with him, lured by prospects of rewards, on different occasions when they saw Vaishali coming clean. They agreed to make official complaints. A couple of them had obscene voice messages, and one of them even had a video. All of them had dirty e-mails. The girls lost no time in lodging formal complaints.

The sick bastard must have been suspended once again by now. Vaishali looked out listlessly at the empty roads washed by the monsoon rains, and the sky kept rumbling.

As Vaishali sat in the balcony, the bottle of beer empty, tears running down her feverish cheeks, she did not notice the man in a rain coat, his head covered by a hood, on the other side of the road. He had been there for more than an hour now, looking intently in the direction of her apartment. He looked down, shoved his hands inside his trouser pockets and started walking further away from the building.

Vaishali Arora had no idea what the next day had in store for her.

Day 22
10:30 a.m.

As Agni and Siddharth made their way through the rush hour traffic, Agni received a call from Arya.

"Agni, there have been a few interesting developments since last night. Vaishali hasn't reported to work today. I came to know some time back. I've been in touch with Crescent ever since. They haven't been able to reach her on her mobile phone either. It's switched off. I had sent out a sergeant to check her apartment. He called a while back to report that her apartment was locked. He had spoken with the security staff in the complex. One of the guards said that he had seen her leave in the morning with a gentleman in his car."

"Vikrant?"

"Now here comes the twist. Vikrant Mittal was suspended by Crescent yesterday."

"What?"

"Yes. Crescent refused to give away details. So I reached out to some of my trusted sources within the company. The girls in the office are more than eager to speak to the police. And to the media. It seems three of the girls brought fresh charges of harassment against him. This time the evidence is rock solid and it's unlikely that he'll get away. And guess what? It was Vaishali who led the girls this time."

"Are you sure?"

"Yes Agni."

"This means she may not quite be the accomplice we've been thinking she is, unless the partners in crime have fallen out for some reason. Where is Vikrant now? Have you checked his residence?"

"He hasn't been home since yesterday. His house is now under surveillance."

"Good thinking, Arya. Though I'm worried about Vaishali. Vikrant won't let her go off the hook easily." Agni glanced at Siddharth and spoke into the phone, "We will need to issue an alert across the city and start looking for the two of them. Keep me informed, Arya."

Agni murmured to himself, "Things often get nasty when partners in crime fall out between themselves, more so when they've been sleeping together."

Day 22
11:30 a.m.

Inspector Siddharth stopped the car in front of a tea stall. The owner, bare chested, had dozed off on the broken bench at the front, the handful of flies buzzing around his head notwithstanding. There was a narrow lane to the right of the road. Siddharth and Agni stopped in front of the third house in that lane.

Agni looked around. It was a two-storey building. The ground floor looked uninhabited. All windows were shut. There was a balcony at the front and a door led to the interiors of the ground floor from the balcony. That door was shut too. The first floor apparently had inhabitants. The windows were open. There were clothes that had been hung out to dry on the railing of the balcony. There was a parrot that moved around restlessly inside a wire cage hung from a rope that stretched from one end of the first floor balcony to the other.

Agni discovered a door on the side that probably opened to stairs that led to the first floor. There was a calling-bell on the door frame. A wooden letter box on the door had 'Gupta' written on it with white paint that peeled off in places.

Agni pressed the bell. After the second ring, an old lady came out in the first floor balcony.

"Who is it?"

Her mouth was full of betel juice.

Siddharth disarmingly asked, "Is Mr Gupta in?"

It seemed the lady wasn't convinced that two policemen had a genuine reason to meet Mr Gupta. "He is not well. What is it regarding?"

Agni spoke out this time. "We are from the police. We want to ask him a few questions and we don't have the rest of the day for this."

The lady disappeared inside the house. After a while, they heard footsteps on the stairs. The door was opened by a man. The man seemed to be in his late seventies. He looked at them through thick glasses that made his eyeballs look disproportionately large.

"I am Naveen Gupta. I worked at the Fisheries Department of the Government of West Bengal before my retirement. Are you sure it's me you want to meet?"

Siddharth stepped forward, "Good morning, sir. I'm sure we are at the right address. We wanted to discuss an urgent matter with you in connection with an investigation we are currently engaged in. I was here yesterday but the house was locked. Can we come in for a few minutes please?"

Mr Gupta did not want to continue his conversation with two policemen standing at his doorstep. He might even have seen a head or two pop up from the balconies or from behind the curtains on the windows of some of the neighbouring houses that almost breathed on one another.

He stepped aside and let the two men in. He then closed the door and led them up a flight of stairs, walking ahead. Siddharth noted he stooped and limped slightly as he walked up the stairs. Siddharth wondered for a moment what old age had in store for him.

"I'm sorry you didn't find us yesterday. We were at a hospital in Salt Lake. My wife was getting some tests done." Mr Gupta entered a spacious but unkempt sitting room and switched on a fan that whirled noisily.

"The rains don't help. Kolkata is warm and sticky pretty much round the year," having thus expressed his disenchantment with the climate of the city, he hollered out to his wife to get some water for the guests.

Siddharth put him at ease. "Mr Gupta, there is no need for formalities, please. We won't take a lot of your time." He took the piece of paper with the address and said, "We are looking for a lady by the name of Niharika Basu who lives in this house. We got this address from the mobile phone company."

The old man kept staring blankly at the two men for a while without speaking. And then he said, "Niharika! There is no one by that name in this house. The ground floor is empty. I used to let that out. But you know the problems with tenants these days. I am too old to handle such rogue tenants. So, it's now just the two of us here on the first floor. My son left us to work in the United States five years back. I'm afraid there's no one by that name here."

The policemen looked at each other.

Agni broke the silence. He asked, "Are you sure?"

The wife walked in at that moment with two glasses of water on a tray. She noticed the perplexed look on her husband's face and asked, "What's the matter?"

The husband looked at her, somewhat helplessly, and said, "They are looking for a Kamalika…"

Agni interrupted, "Niharika. Niharika Basu."

"Oh yes! Niharika. I'm sorry. They are looking for a lady by the name of Niharika Basu. They have found out from the phone company that she lives at this address. I told them it's just the two of us here."

The wife put the tray down with the glasses on the central table in front of the policemen.

"Look at you! You already forgot her name!" the wife almost screamed.

She then looked at them and said, "She used to live on the ground floor. But she doesn't stay here anymore. She died last year in an accident." She turned to her husband and said, "I can't believe you forgot Niharika. Such a nice girl!" Her voice trembled.

The news had rendered Agni and Siddharth speechless.

Agni spoke finally, "Who was she, really? Here, ma'am, why don't you please take a seat here and tell us everything about her. Did you say she died last year?" The questions tumbled out.

The wife obviously loved the importance thus bestowed on her. She pulled a chair and sat down, looking only too eager to tell her story.

"Well, we had let the ground floor out to a couple for the larger part of last year. They were newly-weds. Such a nice couple! The girl's name was Niharika. Poor child! She died in an accident last year in November. The husband was shattered. He left the house. Said he could not stay here with her memories all around him. He moved to an apartment somewhere near the Eastern Metropolitan Bypass. It was also closer to his office."

She turned to her husband for a moment and shouted, "Do you now remember?"

She again looked at Agni and said, "We got a new tenant after that for a few months...a bachelor. He would return drunk every night, play his music loud, bring in women and didn't even pay his rent on time. We threw him out. The ground floor has been locked ever since."

Agni tried to steer the discussion back to the topic of interest. "And what was the name of the husband?"

"We used to call him Ayush," she turned to her husband, "What was his full name?"

The man had the usual puzzled look on his face. He thought hard for a few minutes and then said, "I can't recall his full name but I can find out. Give me a minute."

He got up and walked slowly in the direction of a cupboard loaded with dusty files and books. He pulled one file after another, blew the dust off it, read the cover intently and kept it back on a shelf. After several minutes, he exclaimed, "Here! This is the one!"

He walked back to his chair and looked at Agni. "You see, I was famous in the office for impeccable maintenance of all my files and important papers. I do the same in the house too. See all the files there? They have the rental agreements I made with all my tenants over the years."

He stole a glance at his wife and then looked back at Agni, "She always wanted me to throw those files out and clean up the cupboard but I never listened to her. See, how this paper suddenly became important for Kolkata Police?" He held up triumphantly a stamped paper, which was the front page of a rental contract.

"Now let me see. Here, the full name of the boy was Ayushman Dutt. Such a well-behaved boy! Not one of those arrogant, disrespectful young men you mostly get to see these days. It's all about grooming, you know. He was a well brought-up boy."

Agni looked back at the wife.

"How did Niharika die?"

"It was nothing short of a tragedy. Poor girl probably fell down from a running train. In truth, nobody knows for sure what had happened." The lady's face darkened, her voice trembled again.

"Where did the accident happen?"

"I don't know the exact location. She had a sister living in Delhi. She had gone there for a holiday last winter. Ayushman had stayed back in Kolkata and had later gone to Delhi to bring her back. The accident had happened on their way back. I'm sorry I didn't have the heart to ask Ayushman for more details. The boy was shattered in any case." She was almost in tears.

Agni did not let his surprise show. He stood up, thanked the old couple profusely and then said, "Mr Gupta, I appreciate your impeccable record-keeping. I will need to take this document with me as evidence in connection with the investigation."

The old man's eyes shone behind his glasses. "Sure! I am proud to be of help to the Kolkata Police."

"What is this all about? Is Ayushman alright?" The lady sounded genuinely concerned.

'He is fine...so far.' Agni smiled.

Agni remembered Ayushman Dutt. He had seen him in the Central Plaza Hotel on the night of Sheetal Mehra's murder when Arya had introduced him to the Crescent employees who had stayed back in the hotel after the party. Agni had thought he was around thirty. Agni remembered his expressive eyes, his sharp nose and his chiselled jaw-line. He had been in a crisp white shirt and black trousers with black-rimmed glasses. Not exactly party-wear, Agni had thought. He might have come to the party straight from work.

The reason Agni remembered him was because from his demeanour and from the way the others had been interacting with him, Ayushman had seemed to be the one most of the others looked up to. Agni had smiled to himself. Ayushman had seemed to him every bit the promising young manager the bosses adored and the greenhorns hero-worshipped.

"One invariably finds a few of his tribe in every office," Agni had muttered to himself that night. He now wished otherwise.

Day 22
04:00 p.m.

It was raining hard when Agni reached Abhilasha Apartments on the Eastern Metropolitan Bypass with a team of sergeants. He had collected Ayushman's address from the office of Crescent Technologies.

The northbound traffic in the direction of Salt Lake and New Town was well past its peak. The sky was dark, the tall trees surrounding the apartment complex tossed their heads noisily in the wind and there was a general air of gloom all around. There was a narrow lane adjacent to the apartment complex. It was already under ankle deep water. A handful of private cars sped up and down that lane, splashing the dirty water at passers-by who turned around and shouted expletives at the cars. There were huddles of people, some of them drenched to the skin, taking refuge in the nearby bus stop or under the ledges of the few shops in the vicinity of the apartment complex.

The policemen displayed their cards at the security office. Ayushman Dutt lived in a rented flat in that complex on the tenth floor.

They waited for the elevator on the ground floor for a couple of minutes. When they got in, they pressed the key for the tenth floor. Getting out of the elevator, they walked up to the third flat and rung the bell.

No one opened the door even after several attempts. Finally, they broke into the apartment.

The door opened to a living area. A sofa set was spread out in the middle of a hall with a central table in between. There were a few magazines on the table. The television was on the wall facing the sofa. A wall clock fixed right above the television showed the time as twenty-five minutes past four.

Adjacent to the main door, there was a bookcase that rose close to the ceiling and was stuffed mostly with fiction. Ayushman apparently had an affinity for romantic novels. There was a window right behind the sofa. The curtain was drawn.

At the other end of the room, there was a dining table and a refrigerator. There was a curtain that separated the sitting area from the dining area. That curtain was presently drawn aside. Facing the dining area was a kitchen and beyond the dining area was a door that led to what looked like a bedroom. It was a spacious and well-ventilated apartment, perhaps a bit too big for one person.

The sergeants dispersed in all directions. Agni walked into the bedroom. All the windows in the bedroom were shut tight. There was a door on the other side of the entrance to the bedroom. Agni opened it and saw a small balcony. Looking down, he could see the rear part of the building. He walked back into the bedroom and shut the door behind him.

From the looks of it, it seemed that the bed had been slept in on the previous night, which meant Ayushman had gone out earlier in the day. He had, however, not been to the office. And his phone was switched off.

There was a wooden cupboard next to the bed. It did not take Agni long to break the lock. As he pulled open the door of the cupboard, a heady aroma, distinctly feminine, filled the room. Looking inside, Agni could not believe his eyes.

Inside the cupboard were neatly arranged clothes, all belonging to women. Saris, salwar suits, office-wear, party dresses, night-wear, skirts, ladies' trousers and jeans. Agni took a step back, his mouth gaping.

They could be Niharika's. They could be of the women Ayushman had mercilessly gagged to death. Had all those women been from Kolkata? Had all those cases been closed? Agni had no way of knowing at that moment. All those murders had obviously not been traced to Ayushman – yet.

But, all that was left of those women was the smell on their clothes. The very last vapours of fragrance they had sprayed on themselves. The smell of the dead that now filled the still air in the room.

Agni noticed a small drawer inside the cupboard. He pulled it out and saw a book inside it. Wrapped in black paper. He picked it up.

Agni turned the hard cover page and realized he was looking at a scrap book. Pages after pages displaying macabre souvenirs. Agni's stomach churned as the smell from the cupboard seemed nauseating. For him, a smell or a sound could be far more sickening than a horrific sight. And it invariably stayed with him longer.

Agni sat down on the edge of the bed. He could feel the sweat running down his spine. His eyes went to the souvenirs. There were strands of hair taped to most of the pages. Different colours, different lengths, different women – all dead.

His eyes froze on a particular page. Fragment of a nail Ayushman had clipped off a finger of one of his victims. It was green. That was the colour Medha had worn on her nails when Agni had found her inside the room in her house on that fateful night.

Surrounded by the heady aroma of the beautiful and the dead in that closed room, Agni closed his eyes in prayer. The madness had to be stopped at any cost.

Day 22
05:30 p.m.

Vaishali struggled with the ropes digging into her wrists, her hands and legs tied to the metal frame of the bed. It was not long before she gave up. The efforts ended up hurting her more.

The stench of her own vomit filled the still air inside the room. She felt suffocated. Tears welled up in her eyes. Her muffled cries reverberated inside the room. She doubted if there was anyone around to hear her and come to her rescue.

It was getting dark. She was scared – very scared, unsure of what the night had in store for her.

She felt cold, realizing immediately that she was in her undergarments. She looked around and saw her shirt and her trousers on the floor. It looked like someone had carelessly tossed them away.

Her eyelids felt heavy. She struggled to keep her eyes open. She realized she must have been drugged.

She kept looking around the dingy room, trying to see if there was any way she could run away. Before that, she would have to free herself from the ropes and get to her feet, she reminded herself.

The room did not have a window. There was nothing on the floor, barring her discarded clothes, a few burnt out cigarette stubs and match sticks, and a couple of empty beer bottles in the far corner. There was a door that was shut. There was a square ventilator high up on the wall that opened to a slice of dull grey sky, slowly changing to black. She looked up and saw damp patches on the walls and on the ceiling. There was an electric cable suspended from the ceiling. It was meant to hold an electric bulb but there was none at the moment. The loose ends of two wires spread out from the cable. Which meant the room would be completely dark in a few hours from now.

She had faint recollections of the events of the morning, but had no idea how she had landed up in that room. She did not even know which part of the city she was in.

She looked out of the ventilator once again. Night would soon be descending on the city. It was cold and damp inside.

She wanted to go to the toilet. But there was no way she could. Unless someone came to her rescue and untied those ropes around her feet. She wished she could press her aching limbs together to resist her urge.

Earlier in the morning, same day

Vaishali had barely finished dressing up for work when the doorbell rang.

"Who is it?" the irritation was conspicuous in her voice. A visitor at that time of the day was definitely not welcome.

"Vaishali, this is Ayush."

Vaishali rushed to the door.

"Ayush? What brings you here? Everything alright? I am about to leave—"

"Everything's fine Vaishali. I made a detour this morning dropping an aunt at the clinic a couple of blocks from here. Thought I'd pick up the 'girl of the moment' and enjoy my share of reflected glory." Ayushman winked. Vaishali blushed at the reference to her heroics in the office the previous day.

Ayushman opened the door of his car for Vaishali. It was parked in front of the building, next to the pavement.

Vaishali moved in and transferred her bag to the rear seat.

Ayushman started the car.

"Here…I picked up sandwiches on the way. Care to have one?"

Ayushman passed on a sandwich to Vaishali.

"Thanks, Ayush. I could certainly do with one. In fact, I didn't have time for breakfast this morning."

Vaishali felt tired and sleepy. She had been through a lot over the last couple of days. Vikrant's betrayal, the showdown they had in the office, her getting the girls together, their blowing the whistle on the sexual harassment they had been routinely subjected to by Vikrant and then receiving news of his suspension from Crescent.

And now, the series of questions she would probably have to answer throughout the investigation by the committee. She was in no mood to talk about her 'relationship' with Vikrant Mittal. She had left it all behind her in her mind and wanted to make a fresh start.

It had been raining since morning. The traffic was slow, hardly making any progress. Vaishali was struggling to keep her eyes open.

"Take a nap if you are feeling sleepy. Looks like we won't be there anytime soon," Ayushman looked at her and said with a smile. His voice seemed to come from somewhere far away.

Within seconds, Vaishali dozed off.

For a while, Vaishali kept going through the cycle of half-opening her eyes and falling asleep. The car was moving quite fast now.

She tried to look outside the window, but the road signs were a blur. The streets did not look familiar either.

"Aren't we going to office? Which roads are these?" she asked feebly, the words fluid.

Ayushman did not reply. Even if he did, she did not hear him.

And then a terrible lethargy took her in its grip. Vaishali fell asleep.

Ayush smiled to himself, "Quite a filling breakfast, I must say!"

I sped down Vidyasagar Setu at a hundred, windows rolled down, the wind in my hair, my prey drugged to deep sleep next to me. She would not wake up anytime soon. Her phone was on the dashboard. I switched it off and transferred it to one of my trouser pockets. It was time the world left Vaishali Arora alone. There should be no trace of her.

The rains had stopped but the sky was a steel grey. The Ganga stretched below us on both sides, the gloom of the sky reflected in its black waters. The riverfront stretched behind around Princep Ghat. The trident lights, landscaped gardens, fountains, street food and a quiet boat ride away from the din of the city – the perfect getaway.

Every city has one, I guess. After all, you do need a place to hide when everything and everyone around you seems alien.

Every city has this unique way of killing your soul and then making you shed tears over it sitting all by yourself in a place like this, as if it was all your fault. The smarter among us do not stay content shedding tears. They pay back – even make some profits in the bargain. It is always about who blinks first. I never do.

I hit the Kona Expressway which connects the city with National Highways 2 and 6 leading to Delhi and Mumbai. The concrete around me gave way to the green, and the bumps and potholes underneath vanished. I stopped at the Toll Plaza briefly and then drove straight.

The empty road stretching to the horizon like smooth black silk beckoned me, but I had other more serious business to take care of.

When I had first heard about Vaishali and Vikrant, I had laughed it off. Another weird rumour in the office grapevine. Vaishali was too classy for someone like Vikrant. And she was a friend. Even if she had succumbed to Vikrant's advances, I would be the first one to know. She would come running to me for advice, wouldn't she?

And then I was proved wrong, yet again. I saw them leaving the office together. I followed them, and I stood for hours on the pavement right opposite to her house, my unbelieving eyes fixed on her apartment. Night after night, hiding inside my raincoat. Desperately looking for a reason to be proved wrong. Till my doubts gave way to confidence.

I remembered after an office party, in her drunken stupor, Vaishali had confided in me that she had lost her heart to someone in her early days in college. That in her heart and soul, she considered herself his. Though she had never expressed her feelings for him. Though there would never be rituals and signed papers to bring them together. And there would never be another man in her life. And then, this?

I had no idea what it was all about. Her career? Or just some no-strings-attached romp with the good looking boss? Honestly, I could not care less. In my eyes, Vaishali was no less an adulteress than any of the other women who had died miserable deaths in my hands. There is no bigger dishonesty than breaking the promises you make to yourself.

Over the last few days, I felt the unbearable throbbing in my head every time I saw her. My fingers twitched every time my eyes were drawn to her neck. I spent sleepless nights imagining my fingers around her neck, her hair dishevelled, the eyes popping out of their sockets, the mouth wide open, the dainty tongue sticking out, the drool past her lips, flailing hands and feet, the desperate struggle for just one full breath – one of the several thousands we do not bother to count every day.

Vikrant was suspended from Crescent yesterday. He was now the villain. The system would pronounce him guilty. But then, someone had to take care of Vaishali. And the other girls. That was where I came in.

And then I realized I was fast slipping into a routine. Considering there were years ahead of me, it was time I changed the game. Made it more interesting. And unpredictable.

I reflected on my exploits. What was it about all those murders that excited me the most – now that I looked back on them? What was that one image from each of them that stayed with me for days? And then it hit me. It was the shock in their eyes when they realized for the first time that they were going to die. It was the doomed struggle that they gave up after a while. And finally, it was the anticipation of an imminent death.

What if that anticipation was spread out from a few moments to an entire day? Maybe even more? What if I could just sit there and watch them struggle, fail and then wait in anticipation of death for hours – humiliated, their dignity trampled right under my feet? It would be like watching my favourite moments of the soap in slow motion. The excitement gave me goose bumps all over.

Less than thirty minutes from the Toll Plaza. Almost there.

I left the expressway and turned left. The narrow road twisted and turned through the greens all around, as the wheels waded through the slush.

Day 22
06:00 p.m.

The police patrol car came to a halt. In this part of the city, a BMW 3 Series was a rare sight. More so if the car stood precariously off the road, almost tilted to a side at the edge of a pond, the wheels stuck in the slush. Not a soul around the car, all windows rolled up.

The trees tossed their heads wildly against the backdrop of the gradually darkening sky. They sighed mournfully in the wind that made ripples in the dull water of the pond next to the road. Streaks of lightning ripped through the sky at regular intervals followed by ominous rumblings.

"Get a room, horny bastards," mumbled Sergeant Qureshi as he knocked on the window, assuming the obvious. "Or, are you too drunk to drive? Either way, you are in for trouble."

No response.

He repeated the knocks a few times and walked back to the patrol car. Another man in uniform joined him.

"Sir, it's a BMW." He gestured to the car and tried to drive home the significance of the fact.

Sergeant Qureshi narrowed his eyes and looked in the direction of the car one more time. "Is it? Oh my—"

And that was when he noticed the number of the car. Every patrol car in the city was looking for a BMW with that number.

Vikrant Mittal was slumped in the driver's seat, dead, when the police broke into his car. There was a quarter full bottle of vodka, and an empty bottle of sleeping pills, crushed to powder on the dashboard to go with the vodka – unfailing recipe for death.

Day 22
07:30 p.m.

Arya ended the call and looked up at Agni. "Vikrant Mittal is dead. He's killed himself. A patrol car found him dead inside his BMW near Sonarpur." He sighed. "And no trace of Vaishali yet."

Agni paced up and down the room with his eyes closed, his arms folded behind him. He then stopped and turned to Arya.

"Let's see what we've got here. The call records from Medha's mobile phone led us to Ayushman Dutt. Niharika Basu had applied for a phone connection while staying as a tenant in that house with Ayushman. They had probably moved in together against the families' wishes. She must have needed a new phone number, maybe to avoid her family and her friends who were trying to reach her on her old number. The service was kept active even after her death in November last year. And Ayushman has been using that mobile connection ever since to communicate with his victims to hide his real identity. He is the man we are looking for. All we need to figure out now is if he has any association with Altius Finance to complete our story.

"Get me Raj Lohia on the phone. He's the one who holds the missing piece of the puzzle."

Day 22
08:00 p.m.

"**W**as anyone called Ayushman Dutt involved in the deal with Crescent?" Agni cut to the chase right away.

"Well...Crescent had promised to engage one of their engineers to work with us. We like that about a vendor...when it shows that kind of commitment to a client. And I insisted on having Ayush in the team—"

Agni did not let Raj Lohia continue. He exchanged a quick glance with Arya and asked, "Do you mean Ayushman Dutt?"

"Yes, I believe you have met him in connection with the Sheetal Mehra murder case."

"Well, we did. Very briefly. In the Central Plaza hotel, on the night of the murder. But why did you insist on having *him* in the project? Did you know him?"

Raj Lohia replied, "As a matter of fact, I did. As I told you, I've been working with Altius Finance for three years now. I worked in a number of software companies before that. My last job during that phase was with Crescent. And Ayush was a colleague. More than just a colleague, in fact. We were very good friends."

Agni was now bent over the desk in front of him, a glow in his eyes. "How very interesting!" he exclaimed. "Tell me more about Ayushman's involvement in the latest tender at Altius Finance."

"Ayush was present in all three meetings. Ma'am was thoroughly impressed with his vision and his ideas. It's great working with Ayush. He has always been very innovative. I hope none of the other shortlisted vendors for the project gets to know that I have a personal rapport with Ayush." Raj Lohia laughed at his own wisecrack.

"Mr Lohia, that would mean you also knew Sheetal Mehra from your Crescent days?"

"Of course I did. Everyone knew Sheetal."

"And how do you know that I am investigating into her murder?"

"I read about it in the papers. Ayush mentioned it to me as well. He told me that the police had recorded his statement in the hotel on the night of the murder."

"Did you know Sheetal's husband too, Mr Lohia?"

"I knew he had studied with Vaishali and Sheetal. But he stayed away from the office crowd."

"I can understand. A lot of things change when you are out of college, don't they?"

"They do, I guess."

"Do you know that he too died a few days back?"

"I read about that as well. And then heard about it from Ayush. That was rather unfortunate. In fact, just the day before Abhinav's death was reported, Ayush and I had been in the office cafeteria discussing the shocking murders and your involvement in their investigations. Didn't the papers first report that Abhinav had committed suicide as repentance for killing his wife?"

"Well...that was just a theory everyone found rather romantic."

Arya looked up at Agni. Their eyes met. Agni stifled a smile. Arya looked away. Arya had had a 'romantic' interpretation of Abhinav Mehra's death himself.

Agni bent forward with both arms on the edge of his desk, and said, "And I believe, during that discussion with Ayush, you mentioned my involvement in the Meenakshi Menon investigation as well? My questioning Priyanshi, examining records of Ms Menon's appointments, asking for names of people she had met in the weeks before her death – everything?"

Raj Lohia sounded embarrassed. "Well...I did. Friendly conversations, you know."

Agni came back to his seat, and took a sip of his black coffee. "So is Crescent working on the pilot project now?"

"Yes, they are. Ayush is working with us."

"Which means he spends a lot of time in the Altius Finance office, I guess."

"Yes, he has to. He has to be in constant touch with the users of the system."

"When the two of you are not discussing juicy details of murder investigations," Agni said wryly. "By the way, have you seen him in the office today?"

"Funny that you mention it. Well...no. He was supposed to come down to my office today for a meeting. He hasn't. I've been trying to reach him since morning, but his mobile is switched off. It's quite unlike him."

"Well Mr Lohia...we've not been able to reach him since the morning. He's not home either. And there are a number of things your friend needs to explain. And that's the reason why I wanted to talk to you. If he were to take a day off and go away somewhere not too far from the city, would you know where he could go?"

Raj Lohia was not expecting the question. He sounded unsure. "I'm afraid I can't be too sure—"

The police had been trying to track Ayushman's mobile number throughout the day without any luck. Attempts to track the alternate number he used to communicate with his victims had met with the same fate.

Raj Lohia thought for a while, and then almost screamed on the phone. "Oh yes! There is this farmhouse off the Kona expressway his father had purchased back in the day. No one stayed there. I think his plans were to sell it off for a hefty sum afterwards. I remember we had a few parties in the farmhouse back in my Crescent days. I'm not sure if that house is still there, or—"

Agni was about to say something when Arya walked up to him. He had stepped out a while back to receive a call on his mobile phone. "Agni, I have information from the team tracking Ayushman's mobile numbers. While his office number remains switched off, the other number we have been tracking has come alive a while back and is showing a position on the Kona Expressway near the Toll Plaza to the National Highway 2. He is in that area."

Agni turned towards the phone, "And that's exactly what Mr Lohia suggested just now! Mr Lohia, I need you to be my navigator. We'll start right away. Wait for me in your office."

Agni had no time to listen to Raj Lohia's reply and ended the call.

"This confirms my hunch that it was Ayushman who had picked Vaishali up from her apartment this morning. Ayushman might have found out about Vaishali's relationship with Vikrant, just as we did, and he would not let that affair be buried in her past. Now, why he does these things is for a goddamned psychiatrist to figure out. But, right now it's our priority to save a life."

Agni ran his fingers through his unkempt hair. If Ayushman had indeed kidnapped Vaishali in the morning and taken her to some godforsaken destination in the middle of nowhere, the girl was in grave danger. Time was running out for her, wherever she was. If she was still alive, that is.

Agni pushed the Walther down the small of his back and stormed out of his office. Arya got a team ready and followed Agni within minutes.

This was going to be a long night.

Day 22
10:00 p.m.

*T*he stench made my stomach churn as soon as I entered the room to check on her. She must have puked after I had left to make a few calls.

She lay spread-eagled, tied to the frame of the bed. Her head was turned sideways, the tousled hair covering all of her face. My fingers twitched with their morbid desire. But I had to resist the urge.

I called out her name. All I could hear was a feeble moan. The vomiting had not been able to get the drug out of her system completely. It might take her a while before she was fully awake. I knew it would only get better from there. She had to be in her senses to let the shock sink in completely.

I locked the room and stepped out again. I had to get something to eat. I had a long night ahead.

I could not help wondering what Agni Mitra was up to.

10:30 p.m.

The entire area was teeming with uniformed men minutes after Agni stepped out of his car with Raj Lohia.

"This used to be a single-storied house back in the day. Looks like they had started building another floor on top but never finished the work," Raj Lohia whispered to Agni.

There was no other house in its vicinity. There was just a pond close by, overgrown with water weeds. The relentless croaking of frogs seemed to underline the silence of the night. Dark clouds drifted across the sky.

Agni looked at the house. There was an iron gate at the front. It was open. The pathway that led to the house was overgrown with weeds.

The house itself looked dilapidated. There was a balcony at the front that led to the main door. There was no other way of getting inside the house from the front.

The interiors of the house were dark, eerie silence all around. There were cracks in the walls and plants had grown on them. All the doors and windows on the ground floor were shut tight. The construction of the first floor had been left incomplete. Most of the windows did not have shutters. The few that were there, were tightly shut. The bare bricks seemed to jeer at the crowd that had assembled there at that unearthly hour. For a moment, Agni doubted if this was indeed the right place.

Agni said, "Doesn't look like anyone stays here. Most of the doors and windows have been stolen and sold off."

He signalled to Raj Lohia to go back to the car. Agni and Arya then walked up to the house with the others following them. They tried the main door on the ground floor. The door was locked. They then walked around the house to the back.

There was a half-done staircase that rose from the unkempt garden at the backyard and went up to the unfinished first floor. From whatever they could make out of the layout of the first floor from the garden below, it seemed that there were a few rooms up there, and a narrow corridor ran past those rooms.

Agni turned to Arya. "We need to break up into two teams. I'll break into the ground floor. You take the upper level. Whoever finds the girl, if she is still alive, doesn't wait for the other and leaves this place, am I understood?"

Arya did not waste any time and with one of the sergeants, ran up the stairs. The stairs ended in a corridor that stretched into the dark interiors of the upper floor.

Sergeant Shiv handed Arya a torch as they checked the rooms one by one. The first one had a door that was wide open. Arya flashed the torch inside and moved it in a circle. Nothing inside.

No luck with the second room as well.

At the far end of the corridor, they stopped in front of the third room. It was locked. Arya examined the lock. It looked rather new, not in keeping with the condition of the rest of the place. Arya flashed the torch up and down the corridor to check if anyone had crept up behind them. He then turned to Shiv and whispered, "Shiv, she could be in here. This is the only room that's locked."

Shiv nodded in agreement.

"We'll need to break in."

Shiv got to work and in a few minutes the lock landed on the floor with a clang. With his gun held firmly in his hand, Arya kicked the door open.

Arya grimaced as the stench hit him. He was speechless, unable to believe what he saw as he flashed the torch inside. Vaishali lay on an iron bed in her undergarments, her hands and legs tied to the frame. Her head was turned to a side, the hair all over her face. The acrid smell filled the still air inside the room.

Arya held the torch between his teeth and, along with the sergeant, started untying the ropes.

As Arya lifted her from the bed, her head fell back. Her hands and legs hung loosely. She had not made any sound all this while. She was cold.

"I think we are late," that was all that Arya managed to tell the sergeant as he ran out of the room holding Vaishali in his arms. "The bastard has killed her."

That was when he heard it. The faintest of moans, but enough to keep his flagging hope alive.

"She's alive, Shiv. If we can get her to a hospital right now, she may just make it!" Arya scampered down the stairs, holding Vaishali close to his chest. Those felt like the longest minutes of his life.

Day 22
11:00 p.m.

Agni got the front door knocked down with the help of another sergeant, when repeated threats did not elicit any response from inside the house. As Agni flashed his torch around, he realized he was in an unfurnished hall with a couple of rooms along the left, opening at the far end to another room. There was no trace of Ayushman anywhere.

Agni asked the officers to take position in front of the rooms, one on either side of the door. He walked to the middle of the hall.

Agni pulled up a number from the list of contacts in his phone. It was the mobile phone number of Niharika Basu, dead since the month of November last year.

A moment's silence. A rumble in the overcast sky. The rain came down in sheets. And then, as Agni dialled the number, the silence in the house was shredded to pieces by the ring of a mobile phone from the direction of the room at the far end of the hall.

Agni ran down the length of the hall, the Walther firmly held in his hands. The phone kept ringing inside that room.

Standing in front of that room with two sergeants backing up, Agni flashed his torch inside. And almost pinned to the wall, the circle of light from the torch forming a halo around him, stood Ayushman Dutt. His eyes were fixed on Agni – his hair dishevelled, the blood-shot eyes wide, tears rolling down his cheeks. He looked several years older than his age, his madness written all over his face, as he lunged towards Agni. Agni gathered all his strength in his arm and wrapped his fingers around Ayushman's neck almost cutting off the flow of air. He pushed Ayushman across the room, almost lifting him a couple of inches off the floor so that his toes brushed against the dust, and hurled him against the wall, the gun pressed right between his eyes.

Agni spoke menacingly in whispers, "Ayushman, you've run too far. It's now time to rest. It's not just Niharika's number that gave you away. You love flaunting your trophies, don't you? All those hair samples of your *victims* in your freaking scrapbook. You probably got your kick smelling those dresses, didn't you, you sick son of a—" Agni stood towering over him. "And your dating games on the Internet? And soon there will be DNA reports..."

Ayushman did not move. His eyes were fixed on Agni, his lips trembled as he struggled to breathe. Not a word came out.

With his hand tightening its grip on his gun, Agni prodded it further against Ayushman's forehead. He grabbed him by his collar and bringing his face within inches of Ayushman's, Agni thundered, "Yes...I took it personally, you bastard! I took each one of those murders personally. Do you hear me?" Agni kept repeating himself as he folded his right knee and kept hurtling it on Ayushman's groin, making him buck every time it landed on him.

The two sergeants wondered if they should stop the ACP.

In his frenzy, Agni lost his grip on the torch and it landed on the floor, making the circle of light roll around the floor noisily.

That was when Agni's eyes were drawn to it. Thick red blood on the floor right next to their feet. The source was a deep gash on Ayushman's left wrist. He saw the blood dribble down, forming a thread. A piece of glass with a sharp edge lay not far from where they stood. One of the window panes in the room was broken.

Agni looked up disbelievingly. His fingers curled firmly round Ayushman's collar trying to hold in place his body that suddenly seemed to be giving away. Agni held the gun firmly on his forehead.

He turned towards the sergeants and screamed, "Someone get an ambulance, now! He has slashed his wrist!" Agni fished out his handkerchief and tied it round the wound that was now bleeding profusely.

Ayushman's limp body had started slipping down the wall and Agni's hand gave in to the weight. Ayushman landed on the floor with a thud, his unseeing eyes fixed at the darkness ahead.

Day 23
11:30 a.m.

Agni followed Dr Chowdhury down the corridor of the prison hospital. The rooms on both sides of the corridor housed prisoners ranging in age from nineteen to late sixties, each one of them trying to put up a brave front, most of them broken from inside.

"Our man has been keeping me awfully busy since morning. Everyone seems to want to talk to me about him. The press, the television. You know what I mean."

"I do, Doctor. How's he doing now?"

"A lot better. I'm keeping a close watch on him though, as he seems to be under traumatic stress. I cannot make much sense out of what he says."

"I can understand. Any signs of violence?"

"Nothing at all. You'll see for yourself."

The doctor stopped in front of a securely bolted door with two watchmen with guns positioned on either side.

The doctor left closing the door behind him, as Agni entered the room.

He looked at Ayushman, reclining on the bed. He looked visibly uncomfortable as Agni walked closer to the bed, but remained calm, a marked deviation from the man who had lunged at him in the darkness of the dilapidated house a few hours back the previous night.

The man on the bed suddenly looked weak and vulnerable to Agni. Someone who had already resigned himself to fate. Agni could not figure out what was going on in the man's mind. The man lying there in front of him looked anything but a serial killer, and a kidnapper.

Agni pulled a chair and sat near the bed, as Ayushman's eyes seemed to follow his movements round the room.

Agni looked into his eyes. "Can we talk?"

Ayushman did not reply. He looked outside through the window and asked, almost in whispers, "How did you cope when the bitch cheated on you, Officer?"

Agni could not believe what he had just heard. His jaws tightened. He clenched his fists and closed his eyes. It took him a good few seconds before he could speak again. "Ayushman, you'd do yourself a world of good if you make this quick and easy. So let's get down to business—"

"I had got down to business a long time back, Officer. It took *you* a while to catch up with me. But someone has to do the dirty job. I'm sure you understand."

"You're out of your mind Ayushman. You're proud of—"

"You bet I am! And for a moment I had thought *you* had left the hypocrisy out of the door as well when you walked into this room just now. I was an idiot." Ayushman thumped the bed, cutting off Agni. "You wanted me to talk, didn't you? Talk I will. Because nothing makes me happier than to talk about my art."

And then Ayushman Dutt talked.

May 2014

Kolkata

I do not remember how or when it started. But I realized something had gone wrong in our relationship when within a couple of months I found myself spending my evenings in the office after work reading and re-reading posts on Niharika's Facebook timeline.

Niharika's interactions with her male friends suddenly began to bother me more than anything else. I began to question in my mind the intention behind every single thing she wrote and every picture she posted and the comments they received. I began to read too deep into everything. Everything began to look flirtatious and outrageous.

I stopped thinking about how we would spend the evening after work. I stopped planning where we would head for the next weekend. Instead, I found myself spending more and more hours by myself, wondering if the flirtatious exchanges between Niharika and one or the other of her male friends on her Facebook timeline had other, more serious implications.

Would those men not be more reserved in their comments if she did not indulge them? Did she enjoy all that male attention? And did that mean that she was not happy with me anymore?

I started getting more restless with every passing day.

My possessiveness for Niharika soon began to get the better of me. I started behaving in ways I had never thought I would.

I would wake up in the middle of the night with a sinking feeling and would reach for her phone stealthily to read through the texts she had received throughout the day. And as I scrolled through the messages in that dark room with Niharika sleeping right next to me, I would pray to God that I should not see anything that would break my heart. I would assure myself that Niharika loved me and that nothing in that phone would suggest otherwise. But then, a nagging voice from within would remind me that messages and call logs could be deleted. So there was no reason for me to feel reassured.

On other nights, if she made the slightest sound in sleep, I would wake up with a start and keep looking at her for hours through the night as she slept, to check if she spoke in sleep again and if it was someone's name she uttered in her sleep.

I had never loved or would ever love anyone the way I loved her, and the idea of her getting interested in other men, or sharing even the tiniest slice of her life with anyone else, made me insecure.

I wished I could sit down and talk it over with her. But I could never muster the strength to expose my insecurities before her, maybe because somewhere I was not sure if my fears and my apprehensions were justified in the first place. They were probably figments of my imagination, fuelled mostly by the grotesque experiences of my past. I decided that I would have to get over those doubts by fighting my inner demons myself.

But most importantly, perhaps I did not trust her anymore. There was no guarantee after all that she would be honest even if I asked her.

So we never talked and my anxiety remained bottled up inside me, as I kept spiralling irreversibly down a dark cold burrow of doubts and insecurity. This inevitably began to cast long cold shadows on our relationship.

July 2014
Kolkata

I reached the party in the evening. Niharika had taken a day off from work to be with her friends at Priyanka's wedding since the morning. Some of those friends I knew and some I met for the first time. Rahul was among the latter.

"Rahul, meet Ayush. Ayush, meet Rahul," Niharika introduced the two of us to each other. She turned towards me and went on, "Rahul was in college with us. And can you believe, we are getting to see him for the first time since farewell day?"

"Really? Where have you been all these years?" I asked Rahul.

"Well…I shifted to Mumbai right after college, worked for a couple of years, then moved to the States for my MBA, worked there for some time and I'm back in Mumbai now," Rahul paused, the arduous task of having to squeeze all those glorious years of his life into a single sentence had taken the breath out of him, but not for long. He added, "I'm in investment banking, by the way. It's the buzz these days."

And then, almost startling everyone around him, he screamed at a child on his way back from the buffet queue, who had almost dropped the daal on his suit. "It's an Armani for God's sake! And someone has already spilled his drink on it."

The impending calamity taken care of, his senses registered my presence and more out of courtesy than genuine interest, he asked me "So, what do you do?"

"I'm in IT."

"Ah! Everyone in India is in IT." He turned towards Niharika and asked, "Not the geeky type I suppose?" and laughed.

Niharika took my arm in hers and said, "Anything but, Rahul."

"That's more like it, Niharika. You are still hot as ever and you deserve a tiger!" He winked at me and laughed out boisterously at the unexpectedly vulgar joke. It took me by surprise.

That bout of laughter drew Priyanka towards us.

Priyanka patted Rahul on the back and winked at him, "Rahul, you seem to have hit it off really well with the boyfriend of your old flame?"

And they all laughed out loud, some more of Niharika's friends joining us. I was the only one not laughing. I had no idea Niharika had been Rahul's 'flame'.

Priyanka looked at me and said, "Oh come on, Ayush! Don't look so shocked. Rahul was the one who chased her around the campus. Niharika had nothing for him."

"I wasn't the only one, okay?" Rahul defended himself. He turned towards me and went on, "I don't remember names now. It's been too long. But I was one of the many boys in the campus who had the hots for Niharika but never managed to get cozy with her." He winked again at Niharika.

A fresh bout of laughter ensued. Rahul's confession sounded anything but comforting to me. He went on with some more of Niharika's male friends nodding in agreement, "And why blame us? Our lady here was well aware of our feelings for her, but kept us on the hook for years. She would drop a hint here, flirt a bit there, and lead us on. I guess she got her kicks from teasing us poor boys!"

"We knew that, boys! Didn't we, Niharika?" the girls giggled and winked at Niharika.

Niharika managed a feeble, "I don't even remember what you all are talking about," and laughed, blushing.

Once again, I was the only one not laughing. The thought of Niharika merrily tugging at the heartstrings of a battalion of suitors and enjoying all that attention did not seem too palatable to me. At the same time, not too unfamiliar either. I could relate what I was hearing to what she had been up to lately. I looked at her and saw a coquettish seductress back at her game in all her glory.

I lost the appetite for dinner.

"Niharika, I have to go," I told her.

"You haven't had anything to eat, Ayush." The concern in her voice sounded fake.

"I'm not hungry. I have an early morning tomorrow. I also have a presentation to work on tonight." I cooked up a story.

"Ayush, are you alright?"

"I am. Why wouldn't I be?"

"Tell me this has got nothing to do with those stupid jokes," she asked, almost in self-defence.

"Of course, Niharika!" I tried my best to make light of the situation, "And you don't even know my campus secrets."

She smiled and kissed me on the cheek. "And I don't want to know, either. As long as you are all mine now."

Her lips felt cold and her kiss felt fake – for the first time ever. My mind raced. She had probably lost count of how many boys she had kissed good night after parties all through her *years in high school and college – without feeling anything, just to stay in the game. A good night kiss probably did not mean to her as much as it did to me.*

She paused and then said, "Ayush, can I stay here tonight? They're all going to be here and asking me to stay back with them." She pointed in the direction of her friends.

"Sure. Don't worry about me. I'll be fine," I said.

Rahul saw us and stepped forward. "Aww! What are you love birds up to?"

"He is leaving." Niharika faked profound grief.

"Already? Well...I hope you are leaving her with us." Rahul winked at me and passed an arm around Niharika's waist pulling her towards himself.

"I am," I managed to say.

"Where do you stay? By the way, you guys should see my new apartment in Bandra. You can smell the sea from the balcony." The arm still around her waist, he turned towards me and said, "Come over to Mumbai sometime. The party scene is out of this world!"

"We will." Niharika looked excited.

"Do you have a car? Or should I ask my chauffeur to drop you home?" Rahul offered.

"I have mine. Thanks anyway, Rahul."

"You know what? I'm really scared to drive around the city in my Dad's new Audi. The roads suck big time, don't they? I have no idea what made my old man buy one!" Rahul looked relieved that the Audi didn't have to venture out on the inhospitable roads of the city one more time.

I thought I had had enough for one evening and walked out briskly, without looking back. For the first time ever, I pulled out a handkerchief and kept scrubbing my jaw to remove the last traces of that deceitful kiss.

That night, every time I closed my eyes, I pictured Niharika and Rahul hiding from their friends in a room in that house, Niharika making the most of my absence and basking in the warmth of Rahul's lust for her.

As the night progressed, memories from the past came rushing back to me. Every woman in every nightmare though, had Niharika's face. At times I imagined her, and not my stepmother, wrapping herself around Rahul under a blanket, her face contorted with lust. At times I imagined her, and not Anita, lying on a sofa with a foot touching the carpet, the other leg thrown over the back.

I failed to silence the deafening noise in my mind that kept me up all through that night. My doubts had been proved right by what I had heard that evening. Niharika did get her kick from enticing men and leading them on. The idea of hordes of men fantasizing about her did turn her on.

Niharika was no different from all the other women life had mercilessly thrown my way. The only difference was that I was madly in love with her, which made me hate her even more.

I felt cheated and short-changed and there was no way I was going to live with that feeling while Niharika made the most of my inability to confront her. A part of me wanted to simply walk out of the relationship and leave it all behind so that I could get some peace.

But there was another part that argued that, if what I feared was indeed the truth, then letting Niharika go would amount to redeeming her. And it was not long before vengeance was all that I began to lust for.

September 2014
Kolkata

I scrolled down the lines from the chat.

Rahul:	Good Morning gorgeous :)
Niharika:	Hi
Rahul:	Just a 'Hi'? Is everything ok?
Niharika:	Yes
Rahul:	Hey, what's the matter with you?
Niharika:	I told you everything is fine.
Rahul:	I can sniff something wrong
Niharika:	Why don't you join the dog squad?
Rahul:	Oh come on now! Tell me. What is it? Please.
Rahul:	You came online about half an hour late; and you are clearly not your usual self today. You even started with just a 'Hi'. No lovey-dovey name for me today? :p
Niharika:	I'm fine
Rahul:	Ok that's it…that 'I'm fine' confirms my guess
Niharika:	Listen, if you are not finding me amusing enough, let's talk some other time. It's time we went back to work. I have a busy day ahead. I will try to come online in the evening, or let's catch up tomorrow. Have a good day!
Rahul:	Hey wait! You have to tell me what's bothering you…unless you are too busy even for that.
Niharika:	No dear. You are the one who's busy. I'm the idiot who's probably expecting a lot more from you than I should. I have no idea why I kept waiting for you for close to an hour last night. You must have had other priorities.

Rahul: *Ok. I get it now. This is about last night.*

Niharika: *You get it? Good for you. And yes, I am sorry if I expected you to come online, at least for a few minutes, to find out how I was, after I had told you in the evening how sick I had been. I know you have other responsibilities to attend to. And I am certainly not a priority. Just an ex-classmate who has almost popped out of the pages of history! I should know my limits. I really should.*

Rahul: *Listen…it's not how you think it is. I was too tired last night and dozed off after dinner. And I thought you would not stay up till late either, as you had said you were not well.*

Niharika: *It's alright…it really is. You don't need to explain.*

Rahul: *Please Niharika. I know what you are going through these days. Trust me…you matter a lot to me. You ARE a priority. And I promise I'll make it up to you the day we meet again.*

Niharika: *If that day ever comes. Bye Rahul.*

I gulped down what was left of the whisky and pulled the laptop screen down. That was the last of their chats. I had read all the others over the last hour.

I had decided to stay up to complete a presentation. I was using Niharika's laptop as mine was in the service centre since the week before.

But my mind was clearly elsewhere that night and would not rest till I carried out the plan that had reared its ugly head in my mind earlier in the day. The more I tried to ignore the voices in my head, the louder they got. And the whisky did not help. I knew what I had planned to do was wrong, but I was beyond reason.

As soon as I finished the draft of the presentation, I launched the web browser. Niharika's e-mail settings kept her online all the time and I had no trouble getting into her e-mail account.

She had probably never imagined that I could do that. After all, it was not every day that I had a genuine reason to use her laptop. And even if I did, she had probably never thought that I would snoop on her.

A few clicks took me to her online conversation history. Rahul's was the only name that sprang up before my eyes.

Ever since Priyanka's wedding, they had been chatting with each other all through her office hours and sometimes late in the nights too.

Niharika had been chatting unabashedly with him about the 'crisis' our relationship was going through. In one of their conversations, she even went to the extent of sharing with him the fact that we had stopped making love and that she had been missing the intimacy. The humiliation could not have hurt me more.

She felt I had been behaving strangely since Priyanka's wedding and that she had been feeling ignored and unwanted. I hated the way she projected herself as weak, insecure and sex-starved, resigned to her fate and crying for Rahul's sympathy.

As I read through their conversations, the familiar throbbing was back in my temples and tears welled in my eyes. They had been discussing movies and music and books just as we used to and did not any longer. She had been expressing her surprise at how their tastes matched and how she regretted that she had not bothered to know him better in their college days.

Whenever their conversations bordered on flirtation, I could feel my whole body convulse in anger. The blood shot to my head every time I read Rahul acting anxious and caring in his messages, asking her to eat on time, or checking on her health, and generally, offering her an Armani-draped shoulder to cry on. No one but I had the right to wipe her tears, damn it!

I could only imagine Rahul smell the victory which had eluded him for years. I knew exactly how a man's mind worked. And I also knew that Niharika knew which buttons to press to get a man's mind working like that.

When I walked into the dark bedroom, in the feeble light from the street-lamp close to the window above our bed, I saw Niharika sleeping with her back to me. I looked at the hair tied back, the bare shoulders under the thin straps of her dress, the curve of her hips, her smooth legs bare downward from her knees. And I wanted to kill her. I loved her that much.

November 2014
Kolkata, New Delhi

Niharika had been gone for a week, visiting her sister in Delhi. Her laptop was still with me.

My conversations on the phone with Niharika lasted only a few minutes every day while she was away. I read and re-read her chats with Rahul over the next few days over countless glasses of whisky, almost relishing the intense pain the experience caused. I saw fresh conversations every night, some of them stretching for hours and ending with goodnight kisses.

I knew I was being ridiculously cruel to myself but I needed my blood to simmer, I needed my extreme anger to snowball into something lethal. I had never loved anyone more than Niharika and I never would, but the extreme rage that I felt was unparalleled to any emotion I had ever felt. I was sinking fast. I knew I would never swim back to daylight again, but if I had to go down, I would pull Niharika down with me.

The plan was for me to take a day off from work after wrapping up my meetings with some of our clients in Delhi, stay back at her sister's place for the day and then bring Niharika back home. I could not wait to see the object of my anguish. One had to be hopelessly in love with a woman to hate her the way I hated Niharika.

I spent one suffocating day in Delhi in her sister's house before we started our journey back. That whole day, I hardly spoke to Niharika and was irritable and grumpy with everyone in the house. I knew her family did not like me, in any case.

When we went to bed that night, Niharika turned towards me and ran her fingers through my hair and said, "What have you done to yourself? You look tired and sick. You have dark circles under your eyes. What's wrong with you, Ayush?"

I thought she smelt different. My eyes were fixed on the computer on the study table in the room, the one she must have been using all these nights. All I wondered was if she had informed Rahul that their nocturnal rendezvous would have to stop since it was time for her to go back to playing the loyal and loving girlfriend during the nights.

November 2014
Poorva Express

It had been a while since I had climbed up to the upper berth in our coupe in the train and had turned the light off when I felt a hand prodding me. It was Niharika.

"What is it?" I did not hide my irritation. I was tired. But sleep evaded me.

"I need to go to the loo. I'm not feeling well."

I climbed down from the berth and walked with Niharika to the toilets.

I waited outside as she gingerly walked into the dirty toilet. As the Poorva Express sped along the Nehru Bridge, the relentless metallic drumming of its wheels reverberated through the darkness of the night. The vast expanse of the Son river below looked like a dark bottomless abyss of cold death in the moonless night. The door to the compartment, loosely held shut by a rusty latch till a minute ago, sprung open and the gust of cold wind rushing in through the open door sent a shiver down my spine.

I was near the door, looking listlessly at the river below when she unbolted the restroom door and tottered out.

In the dimly lit passage of the train, in the foul stench from the toilet that filled the air, with her hair dishevelled, her face pale and her eyes sick and red, she looked almost devilish and nothing like the woman I had fallen in love with.

"Why don't we stand here for a minute? It's so suffocating in the coupe. The fresh air will make me feel better," Niharika whispered.

She walked towards the door, holding the walls of the compartment for support, and slid in next to me. She smelt obnoxious as she pressed her body against mine and rested her head on my shoulders. Deceit – my heart cried out. She had been with him on the Internet only a couple of nights back at this time.

"Doesn't it look scary?" The words tumbled out of my mouth as she looked down at the river below. I could not recognize my own voice. It sounded like a serpent's hiss.

"Not when you are next to me," Niharika kissed me on the lips. It tasted more bitter than anything I had ever tasted. Deceit, deceit! She kissed me again. I stood still and did not respond. Cold as steel. One cannot feign passion, and I did not feel the need to, either.

I did not want her next to me for a minute longer. I could feel my hatred and my anger surging through my veins. And it suddenly made me restless. An inexplicable sense of urgency was beginning to take me in its grip. I felt like I had to do something about what she had been doing behind my back and I had to do it then and there.

All my strength seemed to have miraculously found its way to my right hand, which raised itself with a sense of finality and shoved her away from me, right out of the door and past the metal banister of the bridge in what seemed like a split second.

Niharika was too shocked to cry out, though I would have loved to hear her scream and see the disbelief written all over her face. I would have loved to see her riding on gravity and hurtling through the winter air, sucked into a cold, soggy death in the depths of the river below.

I walked back to the coupe and climbed back to my berth. The other man in the coupe was still in deep sleep. No witness.

A few days later, her body was discovered by the Son.

The police asked too many questions.

"What exactly happened?"

"We were returning from her sister's house in Delhi by Poorva Express. We were in the same coupe in the train. I was in the upper berth, she in the lower. She had not been well and I had told her repeatedly to call me if she had to use the toilet or leave the coupe for any reason whatsoever at any time during the night. I had fallen asleep, I had been too tired. When I woke

up, it was quite late in the night. I looked down and she was not there on the berth. There was another man in the coupe. He had been sleeping too and was of no help. I searched for her everywhere. She was nowhere on the train."

"How do you think she ended up in the river?"

"I have no idea. We did find out later that a door close to the toilets in that compartment was open. I know she had not been well. She might have walked up to the door for some fresh hair, felt sick and fallen off the train."

"Without anyone seeing," the Inspector completed the sentence for me, "Poor girl! What a tragedy!"

June 2015

Central Plaza Hotel, Park Street, Kolkata

*A*s I looked around after ordering another drink at the bar, I realized that I had had a few too many. The gyrating figures on the dance floor seemed to be covered by blue mist, the music seemed to be floating in from somewhere far away.

I was beginning to feel suffocated. I would have preferred to be alone that evening in the balcony of my tenth floor apartment with my drink, feeling the wind in my hair.

Through the whisky fog I looked again at people drinking and dancing in frenzy on the floor. I looked at the women – their faces, their bare shoulders, their arms and their backs with a sheen of sweat. I wondered how they smelt. Is it always the smell that sets the blood on fire? Is it the eternal appeal of the feminine aroma that drew those hordes of men around those women? I wished I could grab those men by their collars and talk sense into their muddled up minds. In a few years those smells would not be special anymore. Or those smells would be gone from their lives forever. We would all end up alone – eventually. The whisky always made me philosophical.

My senses were fast giving up. I was finding it difficult to keep my eyes open.

That's when I saw Sheetal once again, looking gorgeous as usual in her pink top and blue jeans, as she tottered towards the bar. She definitely looked like she had had a few too many, too. Vaishali had already left.

The world whirled around me, gaining in momentum with every spin. Sheetal's smile, like always, seemed to light up the smoky, dark, lifeless surroundings. She was struggling to make her way through the dance floor.

"I'm very upset tonight, Ayush," she whimpered, bringing her mouth to my ears, trying hard to raise her voice above the loud music. The next moment, she rested her head on my chest. "Give me a hug."

She smelled great – Sensuous, Estee Lauder. Her usual. Over time, I had come to associate that fragrance with her. I drew in my breath a couple more times, feeling her smell spread inside me, as I did not budge from the warmth of her hug, oblivious of the world around. My heart skipped a few beats and more. I had never been so close to Sheetal before. The world around me spun faster than ever.

I was suddenly happy, suddenly enjoying the ambience, the music, the burst of life on the dance floor. The music no longer seemed cacophonous, even as the whisky further numbed my senses.

I wanted to hit the floor with Sheetal. I couldn't remember when was the last time I had danced with a woman. The music had changed to a slow number.

The bitterness I had been feeling inside began to ebb as I pulled her closer in a slow, languorous dance. There was a storm in my heart – a storm of a different kind. I felt longing. I felt passion for another woman after months, as my arms around her waist pulled her closer and closer to me, feeling her warm softness spread all over me.

"*You are not your usual self tonight,*" Sheetal's drunken whisper burnt my ears as her fingertips drew circles on my chest, and then flicked open the top button of my shirt. As her warm breasts pressed on my chest, my eyes were drawn instinctively to the deep cleavage over the low neckline of her top, the locket nestled in its warmth.

"*Like what you see, naughty boy?*" She winked.

For a split second, my heart stopped beating and the world around me seemed to have frozen. Several months back, I had read Niharika post the same question to one of her friends on Facebook in response to his compliments on one of her pictures from our last vacation in Goa. She was in a swimsuit in that picture, with a sarong. When I had taken that picture, I had been naïve enough to assume that the picture was only for our private albums. I had no idea that it would be up on one of her public albums for the world to salivate over.

Pouring every inch of her body over mine, Sheetal whispered in my ears, "*I bet you'd love to see more, won't you?*"

She disengaged from my arms and let her fingers curl around mine as she walked away from the dance floor, heading towards the exit of the discotheque. I followed her almost instinctively, my eyes fixed on her full hips swaying seductively under her clingy jeans.

She pushed open the door of the ladies' restroom and signalled me to follow her. I was in the grip of unbridled lust.

There was no one inside. We ran impatiently to the last stall in the row.

No sooner had she bolted the stall inside the ladies' restroom than she was all over me.

July 2015

New Town, Kolkata

*T*he only sounds reaching my ears were those of the wipers on the windshield and the rain on the roof of my car. The street was deserted at this time of the evening. Nothing unusual about that, especially with the untimely rains having caught everyone unawares.

I worked from an office complex in the outskirts of the city. The offices here had their own fleets of buses. Once those buses left for the evening, the roads took on a desolate look, barring the occasional bikes and cars speeding towards the city.

Speeding down that road was clearly not an option that evening. The rains were pouring down thick, making it hard to see anything even at an arm's length. I wished I had left earlier.

I was working on a deal with Altius Finance. Crescent had been trying to break into the account for a few months. Vikrant had had three meetings with Meenakshi Menon, the Director of Information Systems at Altius Finance. I was working on a pilot project for Altius.

The meetings had gone well. We had managed to hold our own against competition and Meenakshi was clearly in favour *of awarding us the contract. All that remained to be done now was to make the pilot a success.*

I had always found Meenakshi to be amiable, not to mention very attractive. In fact, I had found out during one of our informal conversations that Meenakshi and I had been to the same school. She had been my senior by a few years. There was, however, no way one could figure that out.

She obviously took great care of herself. She made quite a sight during our last project meeting in her office a couple of days back in her white shirt and grey trousers with her almond-hued hair tied back, the fitted attire accentuating her delectable curves. As she had sat leaning back on the chair with her legs crossed, long manicured fingers on her chin, appraising me with her dark eyes behind designer glasses, she had exuded authority and magnetic sensuality. She had looked extremely desirable and for a few moments, just for those few moments, I had been reminded all over again of everything I had heard about her from her colleagues in Altius Finance.

I snapped out of my daydream in a split second as I almost ran into a car ahead. I pressed the brake to the floor with all the strength I could muster and the tyres screeched to a halt.

That car ahead had clearly broken down. The hood was up. I hated it but the least I could do was get out of my car and take a look. That was perhaps the worst possible place in town to have your car break down in the rains.

I turned the ignition off and stepped out. As I walked over to the front, I saw the same woman I had been thinking about a few minutes back.

Meenakshi Menon was drenched to the skin and water dripped from her hair which she had untied probably after leaving office.

"Now that's a surprise!" She smiled, moving a few strands

of hair off her face and tucking them behind her ears. *"I thought I was the only madcap to have ventured out in the rains!"*

"What seems to be the matter?" I asked.

"I have no idea. She just won't start! I checked the wire connections on the battery and they seem to be fine."

"Want me to take a look?"

"Oh, don't bother." She pulled the hood down and continued, *"I have called the on-road service and the mechanics should be here any minute."*

"Are you sure?" I asked.

"I am, Ayush. Don't you think women and cars are handled best by experts?" she winked. We laughed.

That was one of the most desolate parts of the road. The road sloped down to a ditch on the side. The ditch overflowed in the rains.

There were a few seconds of awkward silence but for the relentless patter of the rains around us. There was a strange sexual tension in the air. I did not know if it was just me or if she felt the same way too.

I finally broke the silence. *"We can wait in my car. I can turn the heating on."* When I heard myself, I thought I sounded too earnest in my invitation.

"Oh really, you can turn the heat on?" Meenakshi winked and laughed, wiping the water off her face. I realized what I had just said had sounded like an innuendo and was rather embarrassing. *"Maybe you can help me get my car off the road first."*

That done, we headed for my car.

Getting behind the wheel, I turned on the heating and got my car off the road as the rain lashed against the windows and the water ran down the glasses.

Meenakshi was next to me, the aroma of her wet body filled the air inside the car.

Day 23
01:30 p.m.

As the nurses walked in with Ayushman's lunch and his medicines, Agni walked out of the high security room of the prison hospital. He was sure Professor Parikshit Roy would find Ayushman's account very interesting. Agni could not wait to discuss the case with Arya and the learned professor.

However, Agni himself was now more uncertain than ever that a death sentence would eventually be read out to the man lying inside the room behind him. It seemed highly probable that Ayushman Dutt would be declared mentally unstable and sent to an asylum.

Agni was about to step out of the prison hospital when a woman walked across the corridor. She was five-foot-something, was of familiar proportions and had straight hair, parted in the middle. For a split second, Agni stopped in his tracks. The next moment, he smiled to himself, shook his head in disbelief, and continued to walk. Destiny had finally chosen to free him from his dilemma. But his sub-conscious, which perhaps needed more time to accept the reality, still kept an eye out for Medha.

The weather this afternoon was unusually nice for this time of the year in Kolkata. Agni looked around himself. He saw happy girls returning in groups from schools and colleges, giggling away without a care in the world. He saw women out for shopping or to catch an afternoon movie or taking a break from work for a quick bite. The city felt safe. He invariably had that feeling every time he nabbed a murderer. And then, another came along.

Agni pulled up Priyanshi's number from his list of contacts in his phone. She deserved to know what had happened in the last twenty-four hours.

A week later

Priyanshi took the call hesitatingly. It was Raj Lohia. He had already called a couple of times in the morning. Priyanshi thought he would want to know when she would be able to return to work. She was not sure herself and had been avoiding his calls.

"Hi Priyanshi," Raj sounded cheerful.

Priyanshi managed a tentative "Hello".

"You don't sound too well. I'm sorry. I called you a couple of times this morning."

"It's alright Raj. We can talk."

"Listen, I'll keep this short. When do you think you can come back to work?"

"Just as I had imagined," Priyanshi thought to herself. On the phone she said, "Raj, I'm not too sure. To be honest with you, most of the people in the office thought I wasn't qualified for the job. Ma'am was the only one who believed in me. Now with Ma'am no more, I'm not sure if I'll have the job in the first place."

"Well, the good news is, you do have the job. You'll continue to work as the secretary to the IT Director of Altius Finance."

"We already have a new Director?"

"You are talking to him. And he has never doubted your efficiency and sincerity, Priyanshi."

Priyanshi could not speak for a few seconds. And then she smiled, tears rolling down her cheeks. "Raj, you are the new IT Director of Altius?"

"I am."

"Congratulations Raj! I'm so happy for you!"

"Thanks Priyanshi. Now come back to work, will you? I suddenly have a lot on my plate to deal with and I could do with some help."

Priyanshi smiled again. "Can you live with the chaos till Monday next?"

"I will try my best." Raj laughed on the other end. "You have a great weekend and see you in office on Monday."

"You have a great weekend too. And Raj—" Priyanshi paused.

"What's it now?"

"Thanks. You have no idea what this means to me."

"Stop being a drama queen," Raj smiled. "You know this job was always meant for you."

A few months later

As Vaishali waited near one of the departure gates at the International Terminal of Kolkata Airport for her plane to Dubai on her way to England, she looked outside through the glass wall. The sky was overcast and there was a light drizzle. The temperature inside the terminal felt a couple of degrees too low.

She was yet to get over the events of the last few months. Her laptop was open in front of her, but her mind was elsewhere.

Vaishali had resigned from Crescent a month back and was on her way to Manchester. She had been selected for a University course, for which she had applied some time back.

When the boarding announcement was made, Vaishali went back to her laptop. The wallpaper showed Abhinav and Vaishali. Sheetal had been neatly cropped off from the picture, which originally had the three of them smiling at the camera at a college picnic.

Vaishali kept staring at the picture for a couple of minutes and smiled. And then she packed her laptop, stood up and stretched. Life was calling her.

Epilogue

A gni went to his inbox to find an e-mail from Rahul.
Over the last few weeks, he had been busy verifying
Ayushman's statement. It had not taken him a lot of effort to
reach Rahul, who held a fairly senior position in one of the
leading multi-national banks.

Most of Agni's questions to Rahul had been about his
friendship with Niharika.

Rahul had been candid about the fact that they had become
close friends during the months before Niharika's death. He
seemed to take pride in the fact that Niharika had considered
him a confidant at a time when she had been going through an
emotional turmoil.

"Niharika was beginning to feel suffocated in her relationship
with Ayushman. He kept drifting further away from her with
every passing day and the worst part was, he never cared to talk
about what went on in his mind. Every time Niharika made an
effort, he would make light of the situation and either digress
to trivial topics or blame the stress at work, though she could
clearly make out from his demeanour that there were other more
serious issues that bothered him," Rahul had mentioned to Agni

during one of their conversations. "Ayushman had practically shut his doors on her. There was no way she could share her grief with her family. They had been against her moving in with Ayushman in the first place. Most of her friends consoled her saying it was a phase that would pass and that she needed to be more understanding. They thought Ayushman was stressed out with his growing responsibilities at the workplace. She bared her soul to me unhesitatingly, because I cared to listen."

Rahul had told Agni that in November last year, when Niharika had been staying with her sister in Delhi, he had written to her mentioning that he had been planning to take up a job in Kolkata and turn over a new leaf. In his e-mail, Rahul had asked her if she saw the two of them together in his new life.

"Officer, you should read her reply to that e-mail," Rahul had told Agni.

Agni realized that this was the same e-mail that Rahul had mentioned, which he had now forwarded to him.

"...I question myself if at any time during our hours of conversation every day, my words set false expectations with you. Rahul, I no longer doubt the honesty of your feelings for me, which have clearly not diminished even with the miles and the years between us. I have sinned if I have unknowingly fanned those feelings over the last few months, when I have nothing more to offer than my friendship, my respect and my prayers for your happiness. I am ready to apologize profusely if in moments of weakness, I have crossed lines I should never have.

I still wake up every morning with the faith that by the time the day ends, Ayush would open his heart to me and we will

*talk and sort out our differences and go back to being the happy
couple madly in love with each other that we have once been,
sharing a tub of popcorn on the couch in front of the television,
or just fooling around in the kitchen.*

*I know you will understand. Just as you have not given up
on me, I have not given up on Ayush.*

*This will be my last e-mail to you. Or any form of
communication for that matter. I don't have the strength to face
you after breaking your heart all over again.*

*Ayush will be in Delhi after a few days. He will take me back
home, our home..."*

Agni read through those lines a few times.

He then looked up from the laptop screen. He saw daylight
slowly fading away. He saw street lights forming tiny dots along
the busy road below, and homebound birds in flocks making
strange patterns on the purple canvas of the sky. He let out a
sigh.

The Colours of Passion

It's a fairy tale wedding – Manav Chauhan, a promising young entrepreneur and the most eligible bachelor in town, and Hiya Sen, the latest heart-throb of Tollywood. Not everyone, however, is happy. The list includes Neha Awasthi with whom Manav broke up a few months back, her father Deepak Awasthi who was hopeful of the alliance with the Chauhans translating into business benefits and Mayank Kapoor, the male model with whom Hiya reportedly had a torrid affair weeks before her wedding.

Within weeks of her wedding, Hiya is raped and murdered in an incident of car hijack.

Even as the hijackers are convicted and the high profile case is slowly erased from public memory, numerous possibilities surface in the mind of ACP Agni Mitra.

After the lapse of several months, when two of the witnesses are murdered, Agni Mitra resumes investigation, finding answers to perplexing questions and unveiling shocking truths in yet another story that breaks into the darkest recesses of the human mind.